CLASHING PERSPECTIVES

Mom took off her glasses one more time to wipe them. She pushed her face close to a picture, as if she couldn't believe what she was seeing.

"*¡Cochino!*" she scolded me. "You like this?"

"Mom, I didn't do it."

"Is this what you're studying?"

"I have my own style. It's different."

She didn't ask where my work was.

"Why can't you go into electricity? Angie's son is fixing radios and making good money." I pulled her away, but she continued, "Did you know he fixed the clock at St. John's? He got his wedding almost for free for that."

I shook my head no and led her to my drawing of striking field workers, which I had titled "*¡Huelga!*" The long dusty line of strikers curled out of view toward a sunset pink as a scar on a girl's knee. I didn't tell her that it was my drawing because I wanted her to like it a lot and then say, "This is really good, *mi'jo*. Who did this one?" But Mom wrapped her Juicy Fruit in an old coupon for Trix and said in Spanish, "*¡Mira!* These lazy people are giving us a bad name."

"Mom, they're strikers."

"*Por eso*, they have hands, don't they? Are they afraid to use them?"

Something dropped like a rock inside me.

JESSE

Also by Gary Soto

GARY SOTO

Jesse

HARCOURT, INC.
Orlando Austin New York San Diego Toronto London

www.HarcourtBooks.com

First Harcourt paperback edition 2006

Library of Congress Cataloging-in-Publication Data
Soto, Gary.
Jesse/Gary Soto.
p. cm.
Summary: Two Mexican American brothers hope that junior
college will help them escape their heritage of tedious physical labor.
[1. Mexican Americans—Fiction. 2. Universities and colleges—
Fiction.] I. Title.
PZ7.S7242Je 2006
[Fic]—dc22 2006041106
ISBN-13: 978-0-15-240239-6 ISBN-10: 0-15-240239-X
ISBN-13: 978-0-15-205425-0 pb ISBN-10: 0-15-205425-1 pb

Text was set in Grajon
Designed by Lisa Peters

A B C D E F G H

Printed in the United States of America

For my brother Rick

Jesse

one

by the time I was seventeen, in junior college, and living on fruit snatched from neighborhood trees and Top Ramen, I no longer thought God was the creaks rising from the wood floor. I knew God was found in prayer, not in the sudden closing of the hallway door just as you stepped from the bathroom. But when I was a boy with squares of black space instead of baby teeth, when the door closed with a sigh, I thought, *That's God. God made that happen.*

I dropped out of high school and moved out of my house because it was scary there. My stepfather drank from the time he got home from work until the time everything funny on television became news or talk shows. At night, Mom leaned her fear on two pudgy elbows at the kitchen table. She liked fashion magazines, Mexican music, plant cuttings rooted in jam jars, and bingo on Friday nights at St. John's Cathedral. No one was happy. There was more music from our nearly deaf neighbor's house than from ours.

I had been lonely in high school. From my seat in Biology, I had paid more attention to the weather reflected in the windows than to the frogs with their legs in the air. Wind blew germs across classrooms. Plumbing sounded in the walls. Nickel-colored water dripped from a faucet. Rain streaked the windows from October to February, and sometimes fog made me stuff my hands in my pockets as I walked up and down the streets I knew so well. Frost put its cold teeth into orange trees and pulled the juice from the fruit. Frost lay on the grass, too, and one morning when you least expected it, the green grass was brown and dead from the roots up. I liked kites in March, but at seventeen I figured that was over and it was better that I begin to think of school and work.

One night our stepfather turned his head from the television, and for a few seconds I could see some of the TV reflecting on his eyeglasses. Indians were falling off their horses, fists of smoke in their faces and rising from their backs. After a swallow of bourbon he said, "Cut your hair."

"My hair is already short," I said without looking at him. I had been sitting in the living room with him because I thought that maybe he would like my company. After he was laid off, no one talked to him because all he did was offer opinions about Russia.

"No, it's long!" he slurred after a moment of silence in which he stared down at the dead and live presidents printed on his TV tray. He turned back to the television when he heard a rifle crack; a shirtless Indian in war paint rolled off a rock and into a river.

"You're not going to be a happy—I mean, a hippie, are you?"

"I don't want to be a hippie," I said, as more Indians fell from their horses. "Jesus had long hair." I waved toward the kitchen where a picture of our Lord hung near the La Palma calendar.

"Jesus is dead," he said. "They lowered the boom on him."

"No, he's alive," I insisted. My hands lay in my lap.

My stepfather grinned so that his small, gray teeth showed. "Where is He? I don't see Him."

I wanted to cross myself and touch my heart. Instead, I glanced at the television, which was flashing the color of spoons and knives. Every house on the block, even the poor ones, had a color TV. But we were watching black-and-white because the set still had a couple of good years in it. When a soldier was hurt or killed in the movies, the blood was gray. When a husband thrust flowers into a wife's smiling face, the fistlike blooms were black.

"God took my good job away," my stepfather cried. "Now I have a lousy job."

"God didn't take your job," I almost snapped, angry that he should even think such a thing. "Your boss did."

He muttered about his boss and picked at some hair snared by his watchband. Then he stared at the wall, where a portrait of a ship on really rough seas hung. It was the most beautiful thing in our house.

After a few more Indians died I got up and went outside to stand on the front lawn and look skyward at one ragged cloud, pulled thin and stripped of any hope of rain. In the east, the mountains rose in a blue haze and the evening dark descended. I looked back at the living room, lit with a yellow lamp. My stepfather was slumped over his TV tray, his whiskery jowls sunk into his chest. He was staring down at the dead and live presidents.

I quit high school my senior year, just after Christmas. My brother Abel, a year older than I and already in City College, helped me fill out forms for spring classes. We moved out of the house believing that if we got an apartment we could finally be happy. We each got ninety dollars a month from Social Security. Our father had died when his body was caught in the rollers of a giant machine at Valley Industrial. We were small, twigs of flesh then, and our relatives had stuffed our pockets with candies and dollar bills. At the funeral I pulled out a Milky Way and took a bite. With my hand over my mouth, I chewed, looking down at the dirty floor. The sweetness rolled in my mouth and disappeared.

Our Social Security money might be enough to live on, we figured, and if not, we could do field work. After all, it was spring. The fields were green with the sweet plugs of onions and beets, with cotton, and the first unraveling of tomato plants. We could drive in any direction and come upon plum and apricot orchards. There were cantaloupes in June. In August, there were the grape fields, which we knew as a dusty hell where you crawled on your knees cutting bunches of grapes into pans.

We found a cottage apartment near downtown Fresno. The screen door was ripped. The windows were grimy, and a filthy line of moss bred where the swamp cooler leaked, but the rent was only $110. The walls were a dirty white, and two doors were darkened with crayon scribbles. Children had once lived in the apartment, and we had to correct their mistakes with paint, window cleaner, and Dutch cleanser. Luckily the landlady, Mrs. Garoupa, who lived with her daughter and her daughter's baby in the adjoining apartment, lent us the supplies. She gave us a bundle of rags, her husband's old

T-shirts—a husband long dead, living now only in the photograph on her TV set.

The cleaning took two days, Friday and Saturday. On Sunday, after I had gone to mass, we brought in our furniture: two beds and two tables. We had a radio but no stereo for our records. We hung up some of my art-work, including the collage of César Chávez and the United Farm Workers picketing for better wages.

"You like it here?" the landlady asked while water-ing a circle of spring flowers sagging in the sun. She was wearing a print dress and a hat with plastic fruit that bounced and clacked.

"Oh, yes." Abel smiled.

We were resting on the front porch, taking in the last hours of day.

"Yeah, it's a nice place," I agreed. I looked at Abel and, poking him with my elbow, said, "Huh, Abel?" Abel nodded his head and said loudly, "It's really nice, Mrs. Garoupa."

Silence ate at us. Fooling with my fingers as I munched on my lower lip, I asked brightly, "When are we going to meet your daughter, Mrs. Garoupa?"

"Glenda? She's away with friends," our landlady an-swered. She breathed deeply and added, "She's not mar-ried, you know."

At that, we sat in silence. We thought maybe she would think that we were too young to be on our own, or wonder why we, and not her daughter, had turned

out well. We excused ourselves by saying we had homework.

I walked around our neighborhood. It was mostly
businesses and run-down houses where dogs crouched
and wagged their tails over the lawn. In time, from
spring to autumn, their tails would clear the lawns of
grass, and bone-dry dirt would be all that was left. The
dogs were helplessly whipped by circumstance. They
seemed hungry, and when I saw one take an orange into
his mouth, I crossed myself and remembered that God
suffered for all of us, even these dogs, their tiny sorrow
leaking from the corners of their eyes.

A week, then another week passed. What I liked best
in our neighborhood was the courthouse, which looked
cool and comforting, with old Armenian men playing
dominoes under the trees. A few of the men sat with
their coats unbuttoned. Some stood with their hands deep
in their pockets, fumbling change and nail clippers, I
imagined. Almost all of them spoke Armenian. I sat on
a bench near them when I was tired from cleaning and
painting, and later, when I was tired from my homework, especially Western Civilization, where I had to
learn the dates when the "great" countries slaughtered so
many for the tiniest of reasons. I sat there, just breathing
in and out and humming a made-up song, thinking of
how I would get ahead, be educated.

I felt good about our new place. It was April and

there were shocks of tiny white flowers in the yard. In my free time, I ran a hose in the flower bed by the front porch and swept away the leaves that huddled by the water meter. One afternoon, while I swept and picked up, I met the landlady's daughter as she fiddled with a key to the front door of their apartment, a baby in one arm and a bag of groceries in the other. She turned and joked, "When you get done, you can do our steps." I smiled. She twisted the key, pushed open the door, and let the baby slide from her arms. The baby took off on its knees, squealing. The door closed.

By the end of our first month I was used to our new place, used to living on my own, away from home. I was used to waking up with the room lit with splotches of sunlight that poked through the tree. The floors creaked and popped, and I liked to think that it was our life, not God, settling down in our apartment.

I usually woke up first, just after our landlady began to move around her apartment. Then Abel woke and, through his orange blanket, a gift from our *abuela,* he would mutter sleepily, "Fix me some coffee. Be a pal."

I fixed instant coffee, the spoon heaped with chocolate brown crystals, and placed it on the table where Abel sat and slowly woke up.

I felt good about school, too. Abel was in his second year of junior college, and this was my first semester. I was thinking I could become an art major by the start of my third semester. I wanted to be an artist, even if it meant that I would have to work at a lousy job to support myself.

I had math and science classes to get through, but I was getting a B in Biology. I was getting Bs in other classes, too, and had almost convinced my art history teacher that I was a good writer. All my papers were written on lined binder paper, my words looping across the page like sailboats.

This was me, a boy getting ahead. Most of our cousins my age were cutting lawns or pounding nails into new houses. Some were pregnant. One was in jail with tattoos riding up and down his body. Abel and I wanted to do something really big. We were Mexican, and we knew it would be a struggle. Mexican jobs weren't good jobs, though César Chávez and others were trying to change this by marching up and down the valley. We would march, too, and we would listen up when our teachers talked.

two

i thought of God almost every day, but when Abel and I went to chop cotton I thought of César Chávez. One day, before it was light, we took a labor bus, a bus with no windshield, from Fresno's west side. It sucked in a hurricane of dust and three sparrows as we rode toward Huron. For nine hours we chopped cotton, each earning sixteen dollars, enough to eat for the week. We stumbled over the brick-hard clods and sometimes twisted an ankle or staggered and fell to one knee, crushing a lung-shaped cotton plant. It was April, still cool and green as we went up and down the rows, not singing because the wind whipped up layers of dust that coated our mouths. For a while, just after the sun rose in a large purplish knot, I hummed made-up songs. I knew slaves had sung to get through their sweaty hours.

Between the hoe-whack and the plants' fall, I did a lot of thinking. Some of my thoughts were of girls from high school. I liked to look at them, but I didn't know what to say to them after my stare moved from their throats to their eyes. I said things like, "I walked by your house. Your rosebush is thirsty." I liked one girl especially, Lupe, a really smart girl who was a year older than me and who was now at UCLA. She was pretty and I knew she never thought of me. She was living away from home, too, and there was a chance that she might do something big before Abel and I ever got out of these fields.

As I chopped cotton, I kept busy thinking about high school. I hadn't been popular. Few knew my name, not even my teachers. When the metal-shop teacher would call on me, he'd yell over the din of lathes and drill presses, "Jesus, get me a one-eighth-inch electrode." Sighing, I always corrected him. "Mr. Boyle, it's Jesse, not Jesus."

I breathed the thick air. I had always wanted to go to England and stand on a cliff, facing seaward. The wind would be clean and so refreshing that I imagined all you had to do was stand there for a few minutes to get your lungs clear. I had been sucking in the same polluted valley air since my birth, and I knew it wasn't good for you. Before you knew what was happening, disease could grow among the velvety tucks of your intestines and spleen, and you would cough up bloody phlegm on your pillow.

At lunchtime, Abel and I kept our distance from the other workers, who were mostly Mexican nationals who spoke a really rapid Spanish while ours was slow as syrup drooling from a bottle. We sat by the canal, our lunch between us, and watched the water flow westward, milky white with chemicals. One fish, gills working frantically, turned like a leaf just below the surface. I felt bad for that fish, a bluegill, and even worse for a frog I saw leap from the reeds, not forward but sideways. I thought the frog would soon be dead, oxygen pulled from its simple heart.

"Do you think César Chávez can really change things?" I asked Abel after I finished my lunch of two tuna sandwiches and an unshaved carrot.

Abel stared at the water. He chewed his carrot and after a long silence remarked, "I can't do this no more."

"What?" I asked.

"Chop cotton," he said.

But except for picking grapes, I told him, field work was easy. All we had to do was wake up really early and then go to bed really early and we would feel OK. Sure, we had to bathe a little more intensely, I told Abel, but just think of the sleep that followed. We made a lot of money when we did cantaloupes in Huron, money that lasted through December, when we bought Mom that copper kettle and that rubber ball with a bell inside for Grandma's dog.

"You're thinking like a slave," Abel said.

"No, I'm not," I answered, hurt that my brother would call me a slave. "This is honest work, and we need it."

Abel shook his head and looked at me strangely with some carrot in his mouth. "Jesse, we'll never make enough this way. They're taking advantage of us."

I looked back at the labor bus, where the Mexicans and one black wino sat dully in the shade with their hands on their dusty knees. *It's probably true,* I thought. *This isn't a good job. Not good enough to keep me from getting my hands dirty.*

I bit the curl from the end of my carrot and remembered when I was fourteen. I worked then as a gardener for a woman on Washington Street. Once, after I had cracked her pond with a sledgehammer and hauled the blocks of cement into an alley, she invited me to a lecture about Mexicans and work. She said that I should come and that my opinion would settle matters. The talk was at the library, in the children's room, where paper flags drooped from the ceiling. White people sat at one side of a long table and Mexicans on the other. I kept my distance, just spinning the globe slowly and thinking that in Alaska the temperature was only 72. Outside, in the harsh light of 3:00 P.M., it was 104, shade or no shade.

They talked about Mexicans. When a lady with a goiter said that Mexicans were pretty trustworthy, especially with orders, if you talk to them really slowly, a Mexican man stood up angrily and yelled at the woman. He said that was Fresno's problem: White people only saw Mexicans as manual laborers. My boss, adjusting her hearing aid, turned to me and asked how I felt. I spun the globe and said it was all too complicated. I told them I didn't know the capitals of the important countries of the world, let alone about how to think of the division of labor.

Before we returned to work, Abel and I emptied loose dirt from our shoes, which were cracked and curled at the tips. We pounded the shoes, relaced them on our feet, and rose with a grunt. The work was slower, and as the sun flashed at the edges of our straw hats, I imagined the cotton plants as kindly people waving at us to stop this butchering. The hoe would rise and then fall, and their skinny arms would drop bloodless in the gray dirt. You had to make up these kinds of things to get through the day. Or you could think about music, even hum some of the music if no one was listening. Abel liked the Rolling Stones, and I sort of liked them, but I knew that some of their music was satanic—or so I read in a newspaper.

We chopped cotton all that day and only once did the *patrón,* a heavyset man with liquid eyes, inspect our work. He was gripping a fistful of papers. He seemed troubled, the lines on his brow filled with dust.

"Are you *chamacos* doing OK?" he asked without lifting his voice.

We took off our straw hats, leaned against the hoes, and wiped our brows. We said we were doing OK, and he stepped over our work without saying another word.

At three-thirty we left the fields and placed the hoes in the back of a pickup. We collected our pay and returned to Fresno with the money folded in our front pockets. As the bus picked up speed on Highway 41, it sucked in a red potato sack, which made us feel pretty happy because it was like a miracle—a red potato sack hitting a sleeping worker square in the face. It scared the poor man and made him cuss in Spanish when he discovered what had hit him. We threw the potato sack around and then settled down when the air became dark with clouds of dirt that we could taste.

We were let off on G Street, a centipede of dusty workers stepping out of the bus. First thing I shook the dirt and insects out of my hair. I needed to wash up really carefully before the chemicals entered my body and rearranged the DNA. I did this at a gas station. I churned the black-handled soap dispenser, and white flakes of soap fell like snow into my palms.

Instead of going home right away, Abel and I bought a bag of *pan dulce* and sat on the steps of the Buddhist temple. We watched people pass, mostly Mexican families doing their weekend marketing. I asked Abel a second time, just after swallowing a sweet clot of *pan dulce,* if he thought that César Chávez would make our lives better. He nodded and said Chávez was a great man, but some of us might have to die.

"What do you mean?" I asked.

"When you struggle, you can get killed by the White House. Look at Martin Luther King," Abel explained. He blew into the empty bag, his cheeks puffed up like the body of a frog when it wants to jump and be in a different place. When he turned to look at me I could smell the sweetness of *pan dulce* on his breath. My brother was a smart person and knew answers to things I was only beginning to think about.

I told Abel I wasn't scared of dying, unless it was a slow death, like suffocating with a plastic bag over my head or drowning with a log keeping my chest down in deep water just as I wanted to come up and breathe. I told Abel that when I was younger I used to wish I had taken the bullet meant for the president—a thimble-size hole in the front of my head and maybe a larger hole in the back where the bullet exited.

A Japanese priest in a black robe climbed down the long steps of the temple. His head had been shaved, and his scalp was bluish. When he looked at us, Abel and I got up and left. Abel folded the paper bag and stuffed it in his back pocket. We walked slowly toward our apartment because we were stiff. We thought of buying a soda but we couldn't waste our money, grimy as it was with the juice of work.

We came to the courthouse park. The Armenian men were not there; a hobo slept under a redwood tree, his cheek to the grass and rough hands like pulled roots at his side.

"Do you think Mom is mad at us for leaving?" I asked Abel.

"A little, I think," he said. "But I'm glad I don't have to live there."

My brother had had more trouble than I had with our stepfather. Abel's hair was longer than mine, just climbing over his ears, and the web of skin between his thumb and first finger had a tattoo, a little cross, which made our stepfather drink more than usual and talk about *cholos*.

So Abel was no longer welcome, but I had to go home and have dinner every other Sunday, just when our stepfather would be wrapping up a weekend of drinking.

We returned to our apartment. It was dusk, the shadows lengthening as the sun pulled west. A breeze was stirring the tops of the trees. We bathed, ate Top Ramen, which we cooled with ice cubes, and then listened to the radio—softly because we didn't want to upset Mrs. Garoupa. We sat on the back porch. The sun had gone down, almost bloodless, and the crickets were beginning to rub their spiny legs for music.

three

monday morning i woke tired but happy, and with my face under the blankets, I said three prayers that gave me saintly feelings. I got out of bed, my shoulders stiff. Abel rose and joked about his sore hands, "the curse of people who hoe without gloves or get nailed to a cross for talking too much." I hit him in the arm for saying this, and he chuckled. "I'm sorry." He knew I was trying to be good, and he liked to make remarks that tested my faith. I loved Jesus more than our mother did, or our father, dead fifteen years now, and probably the color of bundled twigs in his grave.

We ate cold cereal at the kitchen table and talked

about Richard Nixon. Neither of us liked him. He was
letting the country slide downward into an ugly hole.
The world had gotten shabbier. Litter tumbled through
the streets and piled up like leaves against chain-link
fences. We worried that by the time we graduated from
college the good jobs would be gone and nothing would
be left but jobs selling brooms or household cleaners
door-to-door. I was afraid some of the downward slide
was our fault.

"They say in class that we have too many Mexicans,"
I explained. I told Abel how once, in Biology, we broke
into groups of five and sat in a half-circle on the lawn
talking about our feelings. Two times the subject of Mexicans came up. This girl and then this guy said they really
liked the food but wondered if Mexicans changed the
meaning of America.

"They're prejudiced," Abel growled. His spoon
dripped milk as he put it down beside his empty bowl.
A fly, fat with the rubbings of dust that settled on win-
dowsills, circled the air.

"But maybe there's really enough of us," I told Abel.

"You're too much," Abel laughed. "Let's get going."

Our first Monday class was Music Appreciation. We
were wide awake when we got to class, but after roll was
taken, the lights dimmed, and the music started, we
yawned so wide that tears leaked from our eyes. In my
notepad, I drew a figure of a horse standing by a broken
gate. I put straw in its mouth and Abel looked at my

drawing. His eyes now more closed than open, he whispered, "How come the horse is eating pencils?" I didn't stop to explain that it was straw because I was sleepy from the music and had trouble thinking about what Abel was asking. I finished by curling smoke from the horse's nostrils and put a crown of sparks under his front legs.

"This is an unusual Ravel," our teacher informed us as he blew on another record and slipped it onto the turntable. He stood back, smiling, and patty-caked his hands when the music started with a light spring of antique noise.

Music Appreciation was the only class we had together. Abel went next to English, and I hurried to Western Civilization. In class, I worried about the air-conditioning as well as the Greeks slaughtering each other in the third century B.C. Air-conditioning was wasted money. The air was so cold a herd of goose bumps moved along my arm to my shoulders. I gladly shivered through the class, though, because there was a girl who seemed interested in me. Like me, she was brown from her face to her fingers. Her smile was a little too wide, but her blouse was filled with promise.

During class, while I scratched notes with my face close to my binder paper, she drummed her fingernails and occasionally peeked at what I was writing. I wrote furiously, thinking that maybe she thought I knew more about history than the other students.

After my Western civ class, I had a two-hour break. I sat under a tree, half in and half out of the shade. I read my Western civ assignment and I wondered about Lupe, the girl who was now attending UCLA. Was she sitting under a tree, warming herself? Did she have a boyfriend? Did she ever think about me? I was afraid not, even if at that very moment she was, just like me, watching a leaf twirl and catch on the wind.

After a while, I fiddled with the drawing I had started in Music Appreciation. I drew sparks under the back legs of the horse. I needed to practice drawing real figures. I felt that you first had to make things look real, and later, if you wanted, you could do strange artwork like twisting coat hangers into odd shapes.

I stayed under the tree for almost an hour. Then I went to the student union, where I met up with some friends. They were talking about the strike in Delano. Raul said that we should caravan to Delano and join the strike for a day. César Chávez and the workers needed us, he argued. After everyone agreed to chip in fifty cents for gas, it was decided to take two cars Saturday morning and drive down.

"You coming, Jesse?" Raul asked. Raul was a hard-core Chicano who sometimes wore a poncho in the rain. His Zapata mustache was thick; his *cholo* accent was thicker.

"Maybe," I said. "I might have to work."

"Work! This is *la causa, ese!*" he snapped. His

mustache glistened. His eyes were flecked with anger. I tried to change the subject by asking if they realized how the air-conditioning was wastefully cold in the portable buildings. Raul asked me again if I would join them. He wasn't wearing his poncho, but if he had been, he would be adjusting it on his shoulder, a tic he had when he was really angry.

"Come on, *vato!*" Raul's friend Pete shouted at me. He was gripping a fistful of sunflower seeds and flicking the shells in a Coke cup. "Don't just think of yourself."

"I'm not."

"*Pues, ven con nosotros,* bro'."

I was uneasy telling them that I needed to chop cotton Saturday and Sunday. I wasn't sure if it was OK. Chávez had called a grape boycott. Maybe it included the field work Abel and I were doing. I shrugged and said, "I guess."

"You guess? *Sinvergüenza.*"

"OK, I'll be there."

We decided to meet at Pete's house at eight-thirty, and we would all bring sandwiches and a jug of water.

My next class was Speed-Reading, which I had counted on to help me with the other courses. But by the third week of the spring semester, I knew I was reading at the same old speed, if not slower, because the teacher kept asking questions while we read. Did we think we were getting faster? Did we enjoy ourselves? How was our comprehension? All the while we were reading mimeographed handouts on population growth or the power of volcanoes when they first erupt.

I met Abel after class at two o'clock, and we returned to our apartment. On our front porch was a roll of mail and a dish towel, which held a pile of tortillas from Mom. Her note read, "Jesse, you come for dinner on Sunday. Don't forget your dirty clothes. Bring Abel's, too."

Abel opened the dish towel. The tortillas were still a little warm, like a baseball glove when you take it off and put it back on a few seconds later. We went inside. While Abel opened the bedroom and living room windows, I reheated the tortillas on the burner and pasted them with a gob of margarine. We settled down on the back porch and looked at our mail. One letter was from the Marine Corps. I tore it open, my buttery fingers darkening the envelope. It was asking if I wanted to be a man and join them when I turned eighteen in June.

"I won't go," I said.

"Me neither," Abel said.

The Vietnam War was real. Two of our cousins were in the marines, and both of them were really scary; tattoos of naked women crawled on their backs. We figured they were scaring people in Vietnam. We felt sorry for the Vietnamese, although we knew that they could poke your eyes out with bamboo stakes when you were not looking. That was a story I'd heard from another cousin, the only one in our family who had a good job. He had fought in Korea. Now he worked as a surveyor for the state of California. He was one of those heavyset guys in an orange vest that you saw with a tripod on the sides of freeways.

The rest of our mail was nothing interesting. We each ate two more tortillas and drank ice water. After our snack, we went inside to do our homework. I spent some time redrawing my horse and thinking about Raul and his group. I knew Chávez was a great man and I knew that it would be a good thing to picket for the farm workers. But I would lose sixteen dollars, not counting the fifty cents I'd spend for gas. I worried that I wouldn't make it to the end of the semester.

For dinner we sat down to a meal of Top Ramen with a hard-boiled egg and loquats from the tree in our yard. Because we paid rent, we felt entitled to what grew in the yard, especially when fruit dropped to the ground and not even birds or insects were bothering with it.

four

my only class on Tuesdays and Thursdays, besides fencing in Phys Ed, was two hours of art studio for four units, a good deal considering that you didn't have to read or write. The teacher, Mr. Helperin, gave us a project and left us alone. Once in a while he talked about artists, dead ones and live ones, some of whom were his friends. But mostly he sat at his desk watching us.

I first worked on my horse, shading the parts where I thought its muscles might shine in sunlight. Then I began sketching field workers hoeing beets. A drawing like that would make Raul adjust his poncho, provided

the day was cold and he was wearing it. He would say,
"¡Órale, carnal! That's a good one. You gettin' political,
ese." I could draw two workers, like Abel and me, bending over with armfuls of cantaloupes and a lot more mel-
ons behind them.

My friend in class was a guy named Leslie, a Vietnam
vet who was really poor. He lived in his car, a Dodge
Dart pleated from all sorts of wrecks. His hair rested on
his shoulders. His face was lined, his throat red as the
comb of a chicken. His artwork looked like real art.

"That's pretty nice, Jesse," he said, tearing into a
sandwich while he examined the dark faces of my canta-
loupe pickers. What amazed me about college, even more
than what we were learning, was that in class you could
eat and cuss. You could sleep. You could even light up
a cigarette just as your teacher was saying something important.

"Thanks, Leslie," I said. I was beginning to like the
field workers' work boots, which were curled, I explained, from years of lousy jobs. I was beginning to like
the roundness of their shoulders.

Leslie cleared his throat and remarked, "I did apples
once. In Oregon."

"Really? How was it?"

"Not too bad. But cold. Nearly froze my nuts off."

"Just like oranges. Your hands freeze. Did your
hands get cold?"

"Yeah. And I hurt my eye."

Leslie brought his head toward mine. With his thumb and forefinger, Leslie peeled open his left eye, where a dark, ash-colored spot floated in the corner. "A branch hit me. It was my fault. Too bad it wasn't enough to keep me out of 'Nam."

I made an ugly face when he moved his eye left to right and then up and down. His eye didn't look healthy. I stood back and said, "That happened to me once. But it was grapevines. It's sort of like a paper cut, huh?"

"Yeah, that's the way it was. I didn't like doing apples."

I felt comfortable with Leslie watching me draw. He was older and kind. With so much of his body used up, I thought he must be pretty wise. He took a piece of charcoal and paper and sat next to me. He started sketching a village hollowed out by mortar shells.

"On Saturday a bunch of us are going to picket in Delano," I said. "It's for César Chávez. You want to come?"

"Maybe. I thought you and Abel worked Saturdays."

"I'm going to take a day off." I hesitated and then, though it sounded funny coming from me, added, "It's for the cause."

After a while, Leslie said, "You believe in God, don't you, Jesse?"

I was surprised by his question. I rinsed my brushes

and told him that I thought there is such a thing as right and wrong and a greater being who decides which is which.

Mr. Helperin came around in a rumpled white smock, the pockets dirty where his hands rested. "I like what you're doing with the light," he remarked.

After the art studio class I returned to our apartment. Abel was still at school, writing an essay that would get him a B in History. I let myself in, drank two glasses of cold water, and lay in bed, hands folded behind my head. I thought about high school and my friend Luis Estrada, who was probably soaping down his father's Thunderbird and getting ready for a date. I missed him but never told him where I was. I'd just disappeared from high school. I listened to music, mostly rock and roll, and tried to remember friends from elementary school. Those were my best years, when I easily did well in school and thought that maybe God meant for us to play and be nice to each other.

Sometimes I ran into Danny, a good ballplayer, and other times I got in line where Hilda worked the cash register at a drugstore on the mall. She was another girl from the past that I liked. Her fingernails were so shiny pink that I knew she had good hygiene. Hilda was Mexican, but she looked like she might be from Ireland, with freckles on the sides of her nose and some on her cheeks.

I listened to music until it got late; Abel would be

home soon. We had eggs and milk in the refrigerator, and a wrinkled tomato. In the cupboard, we had Top Ramen, cold cereal, and cans of tuna and soup.

A knock sounded at the door, a peck rather than a loud, demanding rap. I looked at our food one more time before I raced to the front door. I was surprised to see Mrs. Garoupa's daughter with her baby in her arms.

"Hello, I'm Glenda," she said, smiling. The baby, in a balloon of diapers, was smiling, too. "I live there. I'm Mrs. Garoupa's daughter." She pointed to our landlady's apartment.

"I know," I said, recognizing her. I opened the screen door and combed my messy hair with my fingers.

"Listen, my car won't start. It's in the road."

"Let me get my shoes," I said. I went in, slipped into my shoes, and hurried out to help. Glenda was on the curb, directing cars to go around her stalled car.

"You get in and steer, and I'll push," I said, bending down to lace my shoes. The car was a Chevy Impala, all chrome and heavy engine. It was ratty, with a mismatched front fender, blue against red. Some of the headlining was shredded, and fingerprints smeared the windows.

Glenda heaved the baby from one arm to the other and, looking both ways, ran into the street, the baby's head jumping up and down on his tiny shoulders. The baby seemed to like this, because he started giggling.

I followed her. When she got into the car, I leaned my shoulder into the trunk and said, "Put it in neutral. Steer toward the curb and don't brake."

She wiggled the steering wheel as the car slowly crept toward the curb. The muscles in my legs burned, and I could feel my face reddening. When the front tire hit the curb, I screamed, "That's enough."

She got out of the car. The baby was grinning, two new teeth showing through bubbles of saliva. I popped the hood and looked at the engine, a wave of stinky heat overwhelming me.

The battery cable was frothy green with corrosion. I wiggled the cable off the stem and wiped it clean with newspaper. "It's your battery," I said. She brought an old diaper from the backseat and said, "Maybe this is better. My name is Glenda," she said again.

"I'm Jesse," I said.

"Is that your brother you live with?"

"Yeah. We moved here a few weeks ago. We haven't seen much of you."

"I've been staying with a friend in Turlock." She looked back at her apartment and said vaguely, "I had to get away for a while."

Glenda smiled at me as I wiped the cable and battery stem. She was friendly, almost too friendly. She was only a couple of years older than me, it seemed. Her hair lay on her shoulders, shiny with sunlight, and she smelled of milk.

When I asked for pliers, she hurried to the house, the baby's head bouncing on her shoulder. She came out with pliers and without a baby in her arms.

"You know a lot about cars," Glenda said as I scraped the cable and worked it back onto the stem.

"Not really," I said. "All guys know this kind of stuff."

"You think so?" she asked, pulling her hair behind her ear. "I've met some guys who can't do anything, even work."

I looked at her but didn't say anything. I got in the car and turned the engine over. I revved it and a ghost of bluish smoke curled around the trunk. I got out and slammed the hood.

"That should do it," I said. I handed Glenda the pliers and then remembered the diaper. I reopened the hood. It was sitting on the carburetor, filtering gobs of hot, dusty air.

"Well, it's all done," I said, pressing the diaper into her hand. My fingers were black and itchy from the corrosion. I couldn't wait to scrub them.

"This is for you," she said. She was holding out a dollar bill.

"No, I can't take it," I said, backing away.

"Sure you can."

"No, I can't."

"You're in college, ain't you?"

"Yeah."

"Then take it."

Glenda tucked the dollar into my shirt pocket. She smiled, pushing her hair behind her ear, and said cheerfully, "I'll bring you something later."

The baby had started crying. Glenda ran back to her house but stopped first to move her sprinkler to another patch of yellowish lawn.

I took the dollar from my pocket. It was creased and warm—and welcome income on a day when I was giving out more than I was taking in.

five

that night glenda came over with her baby and a bag of doughnuts, which all four of us ate on the small patch of itchy lawn. We looked at the stars, our hands cupped around our eyes like blinders. The neighbor's porch light broke up the dark, which upset me because I believed that when it was dark it should be dark and when it was light it should be light.

Glenda thanked me for fixing her car, and I told her it was nothing. She smiled and pulled her hair behind her ears. Sitting cross-legged, fidgeting so that her bottom worked into the grass, she said that she was glad there were people her age on the block. Glenda, we learned then, was twenty-three, almost twenty-four. Abel was nineteen, and I was seventeen. Twenty-three seemed far away, like another town. I wondered if I would have a baby to set down on a lawn and feed doughnuts to when I was her age.

"What's his name?" Abel asked, stuffing a pinch of doughnut into the baby's mouth.

"Larry. It's plain, but I like it." Glenda wiped the baby's mouth with her thumb. She added without embarrassment, "He doesn't have a father. I mean, a *real* father."

Abel straightened up when she said this. I pulled on the grass, bit my lower lip, and wondered where the father was laying his head down to sleep.

"He's all mine," she laughed, playing patty-cake with the baby. She pulled at her hair again and smiled at Abel.

I could tell that Glenda liked Abel more than me. She tore the last doughnut in half, and they shared it, crystals of sugar on their laughing mouths. Abel told stories that made his shoulders jump up and down, things like when he tried to fish a cigarette from our stepfather's shirt pocket while he was snoring in his recliner. The story didn't sound funny to me, but Glenda laughed and touched my brother's arm. I watched them look at each other, and then watched the baby pull up tufts of grass and start to eat them. I softly patted the grass from his sticky hand, which saddened him and made his eyes grow, even in the dark, luminous with self-doubt.

We told Glenda that we were brothers and had moved out of the house to be on our own. Our stepfather was a drunk, we said without much shame. Our mother tolerated his drinking and said nothing, even when he ran his car through the front of a flower shop, a bouquet in his lap when he woke up bleeding from his forehead. For a week a gash stood just over his eyes, and Abel told Glenda that he had looked like a cyclops. We had laughed behind his back, laughed and felt bad because, at the time, we had thought he wouldn't live long. But that was twelve years ago, and today he is still drinking and warning us about the Chinese, who, if they wanted, could all jump up and down at once and destroy the planet.

I tried to cut into the conversation. I told Glenda that I wanted to be an artist, and if not an artist, then a high-school teacher because they didn't seem to work hard and had summers off to think about what to do next. I explained to her that I liked working in pencil, though pastels seemed more like life, full of color that made a person want to look closely. Pencil was like black-and-white television, and pastels were like a big color console. For a few minutes, Glenda was interested, but her smile slackened when I went on to tell about my term paper on Diego Rivera.

Abel said he wasn't sure, but he thought he would like to go into forestry, which made Glenda smile. She slapped her hands on her thighs and shouted, "I like the forest! I camped in the snow one time. I got some pinecones sitting in my window."

"I didn't know you wanted to go into forestry," I said, a bit angry with my brother. He was going to major in Spanish, or so he had told me several times when we lay in bed talking about the dreamy future.

"Yeah, I want to live where it's cool," he said. "I want to live where it's really dark at night. Not like this place." Abel pointed to the porch light, and we all looked, eyes squinting because it was just a bare bulb the color of a really bad tooth.

"I thought you liked Fresno. I like it here," I argued. I pulled at a tuft of grass. I could feel my shoulders droop with disappointment.

"Yeah, but I want to see the world," Abel said.

"In the forest?"

"The forest is the world," he said in a wise way. "What's wrong with you, Jesse? Are you scared about leaving?"

"No," I said flatly. I bowed my head to the grass. Even in the dark, I could see a few ants struggling over the tallest blades, a terrible wilderness for them. I felt I was losing my brother to Glenda, a girl we didn't really know, and in the end I would be left looking down at my empty palms.

"Mom wasn't too mad when I had Larry," Glenda said, with tufts of grass in her hands. "She just threw up her arms and said, 'What's the world coming to?'"

"That sounds like our mom," Abel said.

"No it doesn't!" I argued. "When did she ever say that?"

When Abel turned and winked at me, I pulled at the grass and fell quiet.

Glenda smiled at Abel and chewed most of her doughnut before she stuffed a little into the baby's mouth. The baby's two teeth diced the doughnut into manageable crumbs.

"Do you get along with your mom?" Abel asked.

Glenda nodded. "I know she's fat and all, but she's special."

I crushed an ant with my thumb and didn't say anything when Abel remarked that it was a beautiful thing when a daughter and mother got along.

The next morning, before school, I hurried to eight o'clock mass. Almost no one was there, just some older women and Father Moreno, who said mass without hardly looking at us. The pews creaked and so did the floor and the doors on their thick hinges. I prayed deeply because the more you felt inside yourself the more you could bring to the outside.

Afterward I hurried back to the apartment because I wanted to walk to school with Abel. But he was gone.

My only company was a kitchen sink with a drippy faucet and a bluish fly beating the windowsill where sunlight crouched in a yellowish blaze. The house creaked, especially the living room, and the air was heavy with the moisture of a new day.

I walked to school alone. I drifted through my classes and I thought maybe I should major in Spanish now that Abel was going to study forestry. One of us had to keep the language alive, so that when we saw our *abuela* we could keep up with her complaints about life.

Sometimes when we visited her she would light up a cigarette at her kitchen table and tell us about her first husband, a lowly private in the wrong Mexican army. He was against Zapata, who was a thief in his eyes, and that cost him an arm in one skirmish, then later his life, when he died of blood poisoning after being bayoneted while on the run. It took only two cigarettes for our *abuela* to run through his life, and then nearly a whole pack when she started on our grandfather, a machinist with two fingers and almost all his hearing gone. She was still mad at him over the time he swallowed a metal shaving and passed blood for three days. He ruined good clothes, she said with a scowl. Then the doctor cut open his stomach, plucked the shaving from the lining, and patched him up. When she told this story, her face became clouded with anger and smoke.

I was thinking of my *abuela* when I ran into Raul, who was wearing his poncho and huaraches. He growled, "*Órale, carnal,*" and raised a clenched fist in a *raza* salute. I clenched my fist, said lamely, "*Hasta el sábado,* bro'," and hurried away because I didn't feel like talking politics. I hurried to the west side of campus, where I sat on the grass under a stand of eucalyptus, the wind noisily peeling the shedding branches. I thought about Abel and Glenda—and of ways to keep my brother from her. It was not right in God's eyes. Worse, he could get hurt. Maybe her ex-boyfriend might come back. Abel was strong, but the other guy could be carrying a knife in his boot or a razor blade in his hair. I listened to the wind and thought about my brother. Maybe I could take Abel to the strike, but I thought he would rather work than march up and down getting dusty for no pay.

In Western Civ, I decided to invite the girl who kept smiling at me out for a soda. I decided to use Glenda's dollar that way, a dollar that I had folded four ways and carried in my front pocket. During class we listened to our teacher talk about Greeks slaughtering the Macedonians when they mouthed off about a few miles of ragged borders. I took a few notes and doodled a heart with a bloody spear through its center.

After class, as we started gathering our books, I said, "Would you like to have a soda?"

She looked at me, her eyes clear, and smiled so that most of her teeth showed. She gathered her books and said lightly, "Where?"

"In the cafeteria, I guess," I suggested.

She shrugged, some of her smile gone, and we walked over to the cafeteria, not talking much, though I did remark that I thought the Greeks were pretty bad dudes. I asked her name, which was Minerva, and she asked mine. Then we walked in silence through the leaves and litter.

The cafeteria was noisy and layered with a strata of cigarette smoke. I made a face, and Minerva made a face and said, "It's so noisy."

I bought her a soda, the dollar bill coming back to me in change and a beautiful face to look at when I first took a gulp from the edge of my cup. Out of the corner of my eye, I spied Raul, who was sitting with some heavy-looking Chicanas. He was bobbing his head and saying something to one of them.

"I want to be an artist," I said as we worked our way around staggered chairs. "Let's go outside."

"You're really good," she said, and followed me.

"How do you know?" I took another gulp and then noticed her ear was small and clean, like a flower when you first pull it from its stem.

"I saw the heart you were drawing. It was really real."

We sat on a cement bench, our books piled between us. She took a second sip and then a third. Minerva's mouth became small, and I thought maybe it was from the coldness of the soda. I knew when I got cold my mouth shrank and my shoulders hunched up.

"Are you cold?" I asked. "We can move where there's more sun."

"No," she said, sounding surprised. Then she added, "Jesse, did you grow up in Fresno?"

"All my life. I like it here. My brother wants to move away."

"You have a brother?"

"Yeah, we just moved out of the house."

"Lucky for you. I'm still at home."

I began to tell her about my family, beginning with the death of my father. I mentioned my mother, then my grandmother, some other dead relatives, some relatives in prison, and others pushing strollers around Fresno. I told her Abel and I did farmwork for our money. I told her about chopping cotton, a cinch job because the only time you had to bend down was to tie your shoes. Grapes were the worst, I said, and then told her that Fresno was not so bad if you could find a shady place to sit. I told her I liked to swim, and told her that I was trying to think of God in my daily life. By the time I finished, by the time the sodas were gone, including the chunks of ice, her mouth was no longer small. It was hanging open, baffled by what I was saying.

six

friday night glenda came over to our apartment, this time with maple bars and a carton of milk. Abel decided to help her and her mother collect boxes of junky things to sell at the Sunnyside Swap Meet. She convinced Abel that with his help they could earn thirty, forty, maybe even fifty dollars. Abel had planned on taking the labor bus to chop cotton, while Leslie and I marched for *la causa,* but the thought of easy money was too good to resist.

Then Leslie came by and made our gathering like a party. Glenda offered him a maple bar and Abel a glass of water because the milk was gone. We sat cross-legged on the lawn, looking at the faint stars bleeding their dead light, which we knew was sent millions of years ago but was just now reaching us as we ate, drank, and talked about Richard Nixon. We agreed he had the stubbled face of a frightful crook. We agreed Vietnam was wrong, and that if we could go to Washington, we would stop the killings by forcing the president to listen to us.

But all this talk ended when the baby, trying his first steps, accidentally kicked a sprinkler head half-hidden in the grass. The baby started one of those cries in which no sound comes out for a long time. I knew the pain. I had done the same thing when I was seven, and I figured that if it hurt then, it probably really hurt when you were thirteen months old and had only three teeth in your mouth.

That night Leslie slept in his car in front of our apartment. But first he showered at our place and dressed in the clothes he would wear the next day. I followed him outside to his car, where he put up cardboard on the front and back windows so that no one could see him sleep sitting upright like a passenger on a Greyhound. I patted the window with my palm and said, "See you tomorrow."

Back in the apartment, Abel was out of the shower and standing in his underwear in the hallway, the floor flecked with water. He hummed a song by the Animals, the one about everything being used up by society.

"Do you like her?" I asked.

"Who?" Abel asked. His voice sounded empty in the hallway.

"You know who—Glenda!"

"You gotta be kidding," Abel almost sneered. He wrapped the towel around his waist. "She's got a baby."

"Why don't you come to church with me?" I asked. "You don't go anymore."

"I don't need church. It's a lot of trouble."

"It'll make you happy."

"I'm already happy."

"You could be happier," I said after a moment of silence.

"Drop it, Jesse!" he snapped. "She's got a baby—troubles!"

I tried again. "Then how come the other day you said you're going to major in forestry? You never go to the forest."

"Jesse, wise up. It's just something to say. I don't like the forest."

I felt a lot better after Abel said this. I showered and got into bed, the covers off because with the dark and the heavy thickness of spring weather, a breeze easing the last drops of water off my body was what I needed. I prayed that my brother would not fall in love with Glenda and that Glenda's baby's toe would feel OK.

On Saturday morning Abel got ready for the swap meet. He shaved carefully and patted cologne on his throat, nicked from the razor and, I thought, maybe even a toothy kiss. I watched him leave the house, jump up, and yank leaves from the tree in the yard. Following Mrs. Garoupa's instructions, Abel hauled boxes to the Chevy.

Leslie, awake and fully dressed, decided to join me on the march. We pulled some loquats from the high branches of our tree and ate them on the porch, our backs to the morning sunlight. Neither of us said anything. We nibbled like squirrels and tried to wake up. When I heard Glenda's car start, I tiptoed over the wet grass in my socks and looked on. Larry was sitting on Abel's lap, and Mrs. Garoupa was holding a fringed lampshade.

"I think your brother likes her," Leslie said without looking at me. "She is cute."

I didn't say anything to this. Some really deep air left my body in a sigh, and I could feel my eyes get moist. Not yet twenty; did my brother know what he was doing?

I went back inside the apartment to fill a Coke bottle with water. The day would be long, and I knew I couldn't afford a soda. We locked up and left.

We took Highway 99, the draft of traffic whipping the flowers from the oleanders in the center divider. The highway was littered with burst tires, trash, hubcaps, mufflers, flattened tumbleweeds, and a struck dog with its legs in the air. Two hours later, we were at the Delano off-ramp.

"Delano is really small," I said when we stopped at the first traffic light. There was a cluster of stores and a restaurant, but the busiest thing about them was the passing cars reflected in the windows. I told Leslie it would be really hard to paint this scene. There was too much light, and no one, not even the French Impressionists, would believe such a light.

At a gas station I asked the attendant about the rally. He mumbled in Spanish and pointed down the street, its black asphalt shimmering with the heat of the day. We drove until we came upon a road lined with cars and trucks covered with yellowish dust. Leslie pulled over, revved the engine, and cut it. We rolled up the windows. I took a long swig from my Coke bottle and got out, stiff from the long drive.

"What should we do?" I asked Leslie as we approached the strikers. "Should we tell someone we're here?"

"No, let's just find a place in the line."

We joined the group: farmworkers and college students, a priest in a turtleneck and nuns in short skirts. Chanting "*¡Huelga! ¡Huelga! ¡Huelga!,*" they seemed as hot and dusty as the cars on the side of the road. The line was long, but when it turned on itself, I saw Raul and some of his friends in the distance. Raul was wearing his sombrero, his huaraches, and his Mexican shirt that looked like a dishcloth. He was chanting with his fists clenched. His mustache moved up and down, and his teeth were really white against his dusty face.

As I passed him I poked his shoulder with my fingers. "Hi, Raul." He looked at me for a second and then asked, "You got any gum?"

"Gum?"

"Gum, man. *¿Entiendes?*" he almost scolded as his side of the picket line pulled away. "Gum, man. *Como* Juicy Fruit."

Then his side of the line moved away, and he waved me off.

I looked at Leslie and, touching his arm, asked, "Leslie, you got any gum?"

He searched his pockets and came up with a roll of cough drops, all shattered in the paper wrapper. I put a few pieces in my mouth and stuffed the roll in my pocket.

The police sat in their cars, doors open, eating sandwiches and drinking from their red Thermos mugs. It was lunchtime for them, and lunchtime for the few Mexican strikebreakers who were irrigating the fields. I could see them behind the vines, sitting in the sandy earth, their boots muddy from the water. None of them seemed interested in us no matter how loud we yelled. But I felt proud and sure that if we marched long enough they would see that we were serious.

When I saw Raul approach again on his side of the line, I yelled out, "Raul, how 'bout a cough drop?"

He made a face at me. "Why are you talkin' like that? You're *loco*."

Looking away, I pushed the cough drops back into my front pocket. I felt bad then, a bruise growing inside me. I thought of my brother. At that moment he was probably bouncing the baby on his lap. Glenda was probably pulling her hair behind her ears. He was selling things, maybe a toaster or tools, and when he returned home he would have money to get him through part of the week.

"Are those your friends?" Leslie asked.

"They're from school. You've probably seen them."

"Nah, I don't know them."

Leslie pulled up next to me, his shoulder to mine. He told me to ignore them, and then told me about a dog he'd had to shoot once. It was his puppy, Zero, and the puppy had run into the street and had gotten hit. Leslie said that the driver felt so bad she banged her head against her own car fender. He stopped the woman, and after she left, he picked up his puppy and placed it in a paper shopping bag. He shot the dog with a .22 pistol while it was still in the bag. He buried the puppy under a tree where, as he said, "He could hear the birds sing."

This story didn't make me feel any better. I listened with my eyes turned toward the ground. No one seemed happy, and nothing seemed to happen for a long time. I didn't see César Chávez or Dolores Huerta. I figured that they were back at an office thinking about what to do

next. There was a union leader with a bullhorn, who
now and then gave us new things to chant when he saw
we were slowing down like burros. Another man came
and went with cups of cold water.

The day moved slowly; the crucifixlike shadow of
the telephone pole crawled across the road. We crawled
as well, chanting, and I began to recognize the faces I
passed, those of old men and women, their skin lined,
their hair matted behind bandannas and hats. They were
the faces of my grandparents, who had all been field
workers at one time and who now peeled potatoes or
sorted fruit for a living.

Around three o'clock a truck raced by blaring its
horn. The people in back, all *gavachos,* cussed at us. We
yelled back, "*¡Huelga! ¡Huelga! ¡Huelga!*" Some of us
cussed in Spanish and shook our fists. The truck turned
around and the *gavachos* approached us again, this time
spitting in our direction. The driver's face was red and
his hair was thinning. He looked like our stepfather, just
as he was getting ready to talk about minorities.

"They're pigs," Leslie growled. "White boy pigs."

Raul stepped out of line and shook his fist. He
seemed really angry as he walked down the middle of
the street. His teeth blazed like knives in the sunlight.

A police officer got out of his car and yelled, "Get
out of the road!" to Raul, who turned and gave him the
finger. The officer pulled out his club. Raul laughed and
sneered, "What about it, *puerco?*"

The cop yelled through his bullhorn, "Son, you'll be arrested if you don't get your skinny ass out of the road." From behind the cop car another cop took pictures of Raul, who moved slowly back into line. He smiled tauntingly at the camera. I was amazed by Raul's brashness and upset with the police, but nothing more happened.

We stayed until four. Driving back to Fresno, I drank from my Coke bottle and took off my shirt, wincing at the heat of the afternoon. When I hung my head out the window, the wind took my breath away and made me laugh and choke on the cough drops, the only sweetness for that day.

seven

on sunday my brother stayed in bed, already rich from the money he had earned at the swap meet— fifteen dollars that would get him through the week. He would buy Top Ramen, eggs, milk, tortillas, and maybe even sodas. In the dark I dressed in jeans and an old work shirt and laced up my sneakers. I had colored the tips with green marker one day when I was bored, and now the green wouldn't come out, no matter how hard I scrubbed.

I took the labor bus to chop cotton. For an hour, in the purplish dark, I worked with one eye closed because the wind had whipped dirt into my face. I felt a scratch

in the corner of my left eye when I blinked, and I wondered if my eye was damaged for good. I often worried
about my body and would stand before a mirror, half
naked, to see if it looked OK. Once I had stepped on a
tack in our garage. I wanted to tell my mother or stepfather, but I knew that they would just make a face and
say that my foot was OK, just give it a day or two. In
my bedroom, I had squeezed a tear of blood from my
foot and then a clear liquid that I thought for sure was
a sign of infection. But nothing happened. My foot didn't
swell, and a day later I turned my attention to a finger,
which I had jammed while playing basketball.

I struck the cotton plants with my hoe, at times singing and at times saying prayers that made my step firm
through the rows. I could see that my brother liked
Glenda, and I could see, even with one eye closed, that
I was too young for college. I should have stayed in high
school. My friends were there, and when Monday came
they would go to school, eat their bag lunches, and learn
more about nouns and verbs. They would lean against
the chain-link fence and tell each other over and over
how lonely they were. Maybe when they were drafted,
they would kill someone in Vietnam. Then, their lives
would start and regret would follow them like a tattoo
on their arms.

But I was no longer with them. I was in college and
on the weekend in the fields, where miles of lung-shaped
cotton plant leaves waved in the wind. I plodded over

the clods, my shadow either behind or in front of me.
And I worked alone.

At lunch I ate a sandwich in the shade of the labor
bus, half-listening to the Mexican nationals—the women
they had or wanted to have, and the car parts they would
buy with their pay. Their faces were lined, and some of
their teeth gleamed with gold fillings. They seemed not
to mind the work, though I knew different, because
when we started again, they rose with a groan.

I worked nine hours in the dime-bright sun, and
some of these hours were given over to prayer. I tried to
remember that it was OK to suffer.

I returned home with sixteen dollars, my feet hurt-
ing, my legs stiff, and my eye still itching from the dirt.
Our landlady was sitting in a kitchen chair, watering the
lawn with the garden hose. I said hello, and she said,
"Glenda and your brother went to the movies." She
pointed the hose in the direction of downtown, splashing
water on the sidewalk. I hurried inside to shower and
lay in bed, covers off, my feet throbbing.

Toward dusk, just as I was feeling rested and starting
my homework at the kitchen table, Abel returned home
with a bag under his arm. He looked happy and clean.

"Hey, Jesse," he said as he closed the door behind
him.

"Hey, Abel," I said with my speed-reading book in
front of me. "Where were you?"

"Glenda and I went to the movies."

"It must have been fun."

"She gave us some sweet rolls," he said. He held up the bag and jiggled it. "How was work? You must be tired."

I told Abel that I wasn't that tired, but my eye hurt. That wind had blown dirt into it. Abel looked at me for a second, as if trying to figure out who I was. He tossed the bag of pastries on the kitchen counter and joined me at the table. "Use my hair." It was a home remedy. If you rubbed hair across a closed eye, the thing—the particle—would disappear. He tilted his head toward mine, and I took a lock of his hair and rubbed it across my eyelid. He smelled of cologne and smoke.

"It feels better," I told him, blinking. Abel went to the kitchen sink for a glass of water. He drank with one eye on me, his Adam's apple rising and falling, and said, "I guess you're going to Mom's tonight."

"Yeah, I better."

She wanted to see me every other Sunday because she thought I was too young to be away for weeks at a time. She would feed me and wash my clothes, and ask how things were. Abel still wasn't allowed home.

"How did you and Glenda do today? Sell anything?" I asked. He and Glenda, eager for more, had returned to the swap meet. They had found an ice chest and a swing set in the alley to sell. And they had clothes, record albums, and an Elvis Presley lamp.

"We did OK," he said, almost smiling. "We got rid of the swing set."

"That's good," I mumbled. "You're using your head." I listened to the faucet drip into a cereal bowl in the sink. I shifted in my seat and then blurted out, "How come you're not majoring in Spanish?"

"Jesse, what's with you?" Abel snapped. He pushed away from the kitchen counter and stood above me, his face full of anger. "You're jealous of Glenda, huh?"

"No," I said flatly, not looking at him. I let my pencil roll from my fingers. "Abel, she's got a baby, and she's not Mexican."

"So?"

"So, it's not right."

Abel turned away and washed his face at the sink, scrubbing really hard, and I returned to the speed-reading book. My eyes were wild with worry but, tired as they were, moved furiously across the page. The story was about India. In spite of my worry about Abel, I was glad to know that chickens had spread from India to Bulgaria. I knew why I was in college. Maybe I wasn't too young.

That evening I pulled on a coat and left the apartment without saying good-bye to Abel, who was in the bedroom listening to the radio. I walked the two miles, a shopping bag full of dirty clothes under my arm. I passed Lupe's house. Mexican music drifted from the window, and the porch light was on, moths ticking at its orange glow. For a moment I thought of knocking on the door and asking Lupe's parents about her. A dog barked, though, and I was already late.

When I arrived at my parents' house I stood on the lawn, just beyond the porch. I wanted to run a jagged rock across my stepfather's car, a Ford with a fairly new paint job. I wanted him to get up the next day and in his white T-shirt stand on the lawn and wonder how something like this could happen while he was home. I looked at the car, then the house. I could hear the water running in the kitchen sink. Mom was probably running cold water over a pan of boiled eggs or thawing out french fries. I shrugged my shopping bag from one arm to the other and went inside.

We had chicken *mole,* my favorite dish, with steaming piles of *arroz* and *frijoles.* My stepfather was drunk. He hovered over his plate, troubling his food with his fork, the beer cans lined up in front of him. He complained about his new job and he complained about me.

"Your hair's too long, like a hippie," he snarled after he cleared his throat with a swallow of beer. "You want to be a hippie?"

I ran a hand alongside my temple, and my mother touched my hair and said, "It just needs a trim."

I ignored my stepfather, who had pushed away his plate and was reaching for the cigarette pack in his shirt pocket. I told my mother I had worked in the fields and had enough money for the week. "But I got something in my eye."

My mom offered her hair, which was long and coarse, to rub against the eyelid. But I told her that I had tried it earlier and that my eye was feeling better.

"I hope you don't turn out like your brother," my stepfather growled. His eyes were red, and a snake of smoke twisted in front of his face.

"Leave him alone," my mother snapped.

"Leave him alone?" my stepfather growled. "What am I doing to him?"

"You're ruining his dinner," my mother scolded.

"Who paid for this food? This is my house!" he yelled, almost out of his chair. He took a drink from his beer, one eye on me.

I looked down at my *mole.* I wondered how long he could live. He was almost fifty, and his heart must be used up—a small heart for a large man. He ate and drank, and now he was filled with anger. He went back to the living room, where he snapped on the television set, laughter coming on strong from Red Skelton.

My mother and I sat in silence at the kitchen table. She lit a cigarette and mumbled, "That fool."

"I don't see why you married him."

"I had to. For you and Abel."

I didn't say anything to this. I looked down at my plate. He had hurt us long enough, twelve years, and now he was sitting in his recliner. I picked up a chicken bone and nibbled at a scrap of meat. "That was good, Mom."

"*Mi'jo,* are you eating enough?"

"Yeah, plenty. The landlady, Mrs. Garoupa, is pretty nice. She lets us have the loquats on the trees."

"I'm sorry Abel can't come over."

"He says he doesn't want to," I said roughly.

My mother's face froze. After a minute she nodded and, reaching behind her, turned on the radio. Mexican music filled the kitchen.

I told her I was getting good grades and that I was working when I could. I told her about my speed-reading class and asked if she knew that chickens had come from India. She didn't answer. She looked down at a burn mark in the table. Finally, lighting up another cigarette, she asked about Abel. I told her he was thinking of changing his major. I told her that he had sold a swing set at the swap meet and that maybe he would return to the fields. She nodded, not looking at me, and the Mexican music took over.

I left the house with my clean clothes under my arm and two cans of peas. My mother worried about us eating enough. She offered to drive me home, but I said I needed to be alone, and I hurried up the street. I thought if I walked really fast I wouldn't cry. I ran, but when I turned onto Lupe's block, I stopped in front of her house and let my eyes fill. The television was on. I could hear laughter, but none of it from the people inside.

eight

with abel in the front seat and me in the back, Glenda drove us to school Monday morning. The car smelled of smoke and baby bottles and was cluttered with soda bottles, candy wrappers, some of Mrs. Garoupa's blue rollers, potato chip bags, an armless GI Joe, and a whisk broom. Jumper cables poked like snakes from under the seat.

Larry, sticky with cereal, sat with me. Now and then when Glenda took a sharp turn around a corner, he toppled over like a bag of groceries. He smiled and drooled.

"It's not out of my way," Glenda said with a laugh

when I asked if we were troubling her. She told us she
had to see about a part-time job at the Goodwill Store.
"Jesse, is Larry's bottle back there?"

Larry was licking the inside of a Butterfinger candy
wrapper. I searched the seat near me for a bottle.

"No, I don't see it," I told her. I picked up the
GI Joe and handed it to the baby, who put it in his
mouth feet first.

I wasn't upset with either Abel or Glenda. After I
had returned from Sunday dinner, Abel had promised
he would keep his distance from Glenda. We even
prayed together, each at our own bed, and when we finished Abel suggested that we go on a vacation. Spring
break was only a week away. He figured that if we could
maybe get an extra twenty dollars, we could hitchhike to
Pismo Beach. We talked about it in the dark, and even
after Abel fell asleep, I thought about the sea and why
God made it first. I fell asleep feeling at peace.

The next morning, Abel and I got some more sleep
in Music Appreciation while something by Bach played.
Toward the end of the class, the teacher gave us a pop
quiz. I figured that I got about half right, which would
most likely be a C on the curve because none of our
classmates knew anything. Abel got only five or six right,
he thought. I was surprised by this because my brother
was good at remembering songs. But he slept more in

class and didn't hear enough music to get the same score as me.

Then I went to Western Civ, the class with air-conditioning that pulled chills from my body. I listened some but I spent most of my time thinking of Minerva. I knew she wasn't smart. If she was in my music appreciation class, she would probably bring down the curve and I would end up with a B or higher. After class, we left together, she with her books pressed to her chest. I asked about her weekend, and she said that her boyfriend had returned home from the service.

"You have a boyfriend?" I asked, stopping in my tracks. A lump of sorrow formed in my throat, and when I swallowed, some of the sorrow dripped into my stomach. I felt betrayed because I had thought she was starting to like me. She'd smiled at me a couple of times in class and even asked if my middle name was Anthony because, she had said, I looked like a cousin of hers from East L.A.

"Well, he's not *really* my boyfriend," she said skipping over a puddle on the walkway. Maybe she was testing me. Maybe she wanted me to say that I didn't have a girlfriend.

"Then who is he?" I asked, the lump in my throat melting.

"A guy I met last year. He's in the reserves."

We started walking again, and she told me that she

had met him at Woolworth's. He was the assistant manager and only twenty-six.

"Do you like him?" I asked. The lump grew back, and my voice almost cracked when I asked, "Is he good-looking?"

"No, not really," she said, but her voice jumped when she said it. "But he is nice."

I wanted to tell her that I was nice, too, but I couldn't get the words out. I wasn't feeling very good, and I felt worse when I saw Raul swaggering out of the commons, dressed in his huaraches, his serape, his Mexican dishrag shirt, and worn jeans. He didn't look like he belonged in college.

"Hey, Jesse, you left too early!" he yelled as he approached us. "Man, we got into it with those *gavachos.*"

"You got in a fight?"

"Nah, we just looked at each other. We bought some sodas in Delano, and *pues,* they were there putting a new battery in their truck."

Raul turned a smile on Minerva and said, "Check you out. Is this your first year?"

Minerva looked down at her shoes and smiled. "Yeah. I'm from McClane."

I said reluctantly, "This is Minerva. She's in my Western civ class."

"*Pues, mucho gusto,*" Raul said, turning on his charm. He extended his hand, and when Minerva extended hers, I could smell her perfume. She looked beautiful. Her teeth were white and almost straight. Her chewing gum glistened like a jewel on her back molars.

"You want to join MEChA?" Raul asked. "Give it some thought." Turning to me, he reminded me of the meeting at Jesus's apartment. He said that I could bring Leslie if I wanted. "The brother's OK for a white guy," Raul said.

"Yeah, he picked apples in Washington," I said.

"*Órale,* he's on our side, bro'. Check you later."

Minerva and I spent an hour talking about the boy who wasn't really her boyfriend. I learned that he could parachute and was thinking of going back to school to study electricity. He also danced in a *folklórico* group.

Afterward, I left for Speed-Reading and felt that my eyes didn't work that well because they kept getting stuck on easy words. I began to think that maybe the dirt from the fields had ruined them. But when I looked around the room, all the students were moving their lips really fast. Right then I began to think that maybe they were all using their mouths more than their eyes, and that I should do the same. We read the passage about the chickens that had walked from India to Bulgaria. We read it in three minutes and then took a quiz, our eyes and mouths really going to work.

I waited for Abel after my speed-reading class, but he had to stay for a tutorial in math, and I left feeling low. I only began to feel better when I remembered that

Abel had promised to stay away from Glenda, and that we were also going to Pismo Beach. It had been years since we'd run handfuls of sand through our fingers and let the waves lick our legs.

When I arrived at the apartment, Mrs. Garoupa was sitting on the ground. She looked like Humpty Dumpty after he fell from the wall.

"Are you hurt?" I asked.

"Hurt?" she asked, her face puckered. "I'm just cleaning around the sprinklers."

I saw she had a pair of shiny scissors and a paper bag. She was clipping back the scraggly Bermuda grass.

"And look, I found all this change." She worked a trembling hand into her apron and brought out some dirt-caked coins. Bending over, I looked closely at a quarter, three nickels, and an army of pennies.

"Guess what?"

"What?"

"Glenda got the job at Goodwill."

I nodded and smiled at this news and went inside our apartment. I opened the refrigerator, looked at the milk, cheese, and tortillas, and closed it again. I thought about our vacation and the extra money we needed. Maybe I could find something in the alleys to sell. Abel had found a swing set and an ice chest; maybe I could dig up something.

In an alley I searched among the discarded boxes and

behind filthy mattresses propped up against fences. I looked carefully because I was scared of spiders, rats, and anything with fangs. I found a tricycle without tires or handlebars, a blow-up swimming pool, a lawn chair with no webbing, and a soggy bag of lawn fertilizer, just about everything a father or stepfather would throw over a fence. I found a tottering pile of rain-warped magazines and a step stool. I found a carton of unused nails, a trowel, and a beach towel with the print of a pretty Hawaiian woman in a grass skirt. I held up the towel, which was splotched with a bleach mark, and threw it over my arm.

I had spent an hour looking for stuff before I came upon a dog.

"Hey, pooch," I called, snapping my fingers.

The dog looked at me with milky eyes. I knelt down and ran a hand over his head, pulling his skin so that his eyes became narrow, almost as if a wind was blowing in his face. The dog followed me up and down the alley, and then trotted away, his nails clicking on the asphalt like typewriter keys.

I dragged some of the stuff back to the apartment and decided, with Mrs. Garoupa's permission, to have a yard sale the next day after school. I had to go back for my major find—a small TV set, the kind our grandfather had watched alone in the garage.

When I returned home for the final time, Abel was

scrubbing his dirty clothes in the bathtub. He had the radio on and jumped when I yelled, "Abel! Look what I got!"

He sighed. "I thought you were Mom."

I shook my head. "Come on." He followed me, his hands covered with soapsuds. He was excited by my finds, especially the TV. We dusted it off, plugged it in, and jumped when there was a snap and Walter Cronkite's face, twisted with static, looked seriously at us. He said there was heavy shooting outside Hanoi.

The next day after school, Abel and I hurried home and set our goods on the front lawn. Glenda brought out a box of paperback books to sell, and her mom unfolded a card table and set some junk on it—salt and pepper shakers, a picture of Lawrence Welk, a yo-yo, some new shoelaces, a quilt, and an assortment of plates.

"It's like a party," Glenda said, pulling her hair behind her ear.

"Yeah," Abel shouted from Mrs. Garoupa's window, where he was running an extension cord from her apartment. He turned on the television and worked the rabbit ears until "The Flintstones" came in clear. Dino, their dinosaur dog, was burying a bone in the yard.

"Did you have a rough day at school?" Glenda asked Abel. She had brought over a bag of cookies and was offering them around.

"Nah, just a regular day," Abel said, and waved off the cookies with a "no, thanks."

"I got that job at Goodwill." She looked around at our spread of things and remarked, "This is all pretty junky. Not like what's at Goodwill."

"Yeah, but me and Jesse are going to Pismo. We just need a little more money."

Abel had definitely cooled on Glenda. I could see that Glenda's baby, his big toe still bandaged from when he had kicked the sprinkler head, was now walking. Squealing, he tottered over the lawn, fell, got up, and tottered again. He was wildly happy to get going.

I bought the shoelaces from Mrs. Garoupa, which made her laugh out loud because she was able to make change with the money she had found on the lawn. And she bought the blow-up swimming pool for Larry.

In the end, after bargaining with each other—and with a few people who passed by—Abel and I came out twenty-seven dollars ahead. We sold the television to a man returning home from work with lamb chops under his arm.

nine

i loved the sea in any kind of weather, and I loved standing by the road with my thumb out, too. Abel and I were on Highway 41 with food, a change of clothes each, blankets, and a sleeping bag I had borrowed from Leslie. He had given us a ride to the outskirts of Fresno and offered us an unfinished bag of sunflower seeds. He drove away, his engine popping, and at a quarter to nine on Friday morning we were on spring break.

We stood on the country road for two hours, kicking gravel, gazing down the road for oncoming cars, and wondering how long before our stepfather stubbed out his last cigarette and let his head drop onto his chest.

"I'm worried about Mom," I said to Abel.

Wind was whipping his hair into his eyes.

"Why? She's got a job. The car's almost new."

Abel made sense. Mom and our stepfather had a new used car, and after six years, Mom had moved from peeling potatoes to a job in an office. She was the person on the other end of the telephone who said, "Customer service."

"I wish he was different," I said of our stepfather. "Remember when he played basketball with us?"

"Yeah."

"It was fun, huh?"

"Yeah."

"He didn't seem that mean." I tossed a handful of seed, and sparrows, the color of gravel, dropped from the barbed-wire fence and scattered for it.

If Abel and I stayed in college long enough, maybe we could earn enough money to buy our mother back, to buy her something more than the glare of a TV on Friday nights.

Finally, just before noon, a rattling truck stopped in a cloud of dust. The driver yelled, "Where you fellas going?"

"Pismo Beach!" we screamed. We raced to his truck and jumped in the back among the rope, shovels, hoes, rakes, wood stakes, and a red gas can—all splattered with mud.

We liked the wind in our hair. We liked seeing the

farms rush past us, with cows and horses grazing on stubble and an occasional dog running wildly in circles. Some children waved and others just looked at us, their hands at their sides. When I leaned over the edge of the truck, my mouth filled and choked with air.

"Do you think it'll be cold?" I yelled to Abel.

"What?" he shouted as he leaned toward me.

"I said, do you think it'll be cold?"

"What? I can't hear you." Abel put his ear to my mouth, and I screamed, "This is fun, huh?"

He nodded.

It was more than fun. It was an honest-to-goodness adventure. Riding in the truck, with our words whipped every which way, was like being on the labor bus, except we didn't have to go to work. We were headed toward the sea. I had brought a fistful of colored pencils and rolls of paper. I could see inside my head a crashing sea and a slick walrus on a rock, his mustache dripping downward. I wanted to sketch seagulls, waves breaking on rocks, sand crabs, and sea otters on their backs. While Abel listened to his music, I closed my eyes and pictured waves rocking, a lazy light inside my head.

The farmer left us off near Stratford. We thanked him, and he drove off in the same cloud of dust he had stopped in thirty miles earlier. We stood on the side of the road. The horizon was a thin pencil marking in the east. Some birds flapped down on the barbed-wire fence and looked at us, their beaks open. Highway 41 was as empty as the inside of a hat.

"Where is everyone?" I asked. My words were picked up by the April wind and rushed away, maybe dropped in the yellow weeds where snakes and gophers struggled over a meager living.

Highway 41 led to the sea, but on a Friday most people were going to work. When a car passed, we hooked our thumbs. Dust swirled around our faces and gravel crept a few inches toward the sea. We sat down on our blankets and sleeping bag and waited for a ride.

"Where would you really like to go?" I asked Abel, who was pinching a sliver from the web of skin between his thumb and index finger.

"What do you mean?"

"I mean, where would you really, really, really like to go?"

By my fourth explanation and by the time he had gotten the sliver out, Abel finally understood what I was talking about. He told me that he would like to join me on a canoe trip up the Amazon. He heard that you could drink straight from the river and that the Indians were really friendly. I told him that I would like to go to Ireland and spend a summer in a stone hut with a thatched roof.

"That's a cool dream," Abel said.

A car stopped, and the driver rolled down the window. "Where you boys headed?" He whistled between gapped teeth.

"Pismo Beach," we said as we gathered our things and threw them in the backseat of his Dodge Dart. We climbed into the front seat.

"It can get lonely out there," he said with a smile.

We nodded, and the car pulled away, its tires kicking the gravel back again, away from the sea.

"Where you boys from?" the man asked after he got the car up to cruising speed. He was small, almost too small to drive a car, and he was sitting on a pillow. He craned his neck to see over the dash.

"We're from Fresno," Abel said.

"I'm from Visalia. I'm a salesman. I sell watches and things. You boys interested in watches?" He gazed down at his briefcase and opened it with one hand. Its contents gleamed. When I looked closely, I saw that each of the watches read a different time.

"They're pretty," I said, petting the face of a Timex.

"What can I do to make you a deal?" he asked.

"We don't have any money."

The small man didn't say anything for a moment and then chuckled, "Me neither." He closed the briefcase and told us he was born in Tulsa but raised in Oildale. We expected more of his life story, but he drove in silence, playing with the wing window. Then he asked, "You boys interested in rings? Girls like rings. You like girls?"

"Yeah, we like girls."

"Yeah, we really like girls," I said. "But they're difficult to find."

"No, not for two handsome boys like you. I don't believe it."

"It's true," I said.

"You fellas could be lifeguards. The girls are probably hugging their pillows right now for you."

I almost blushed when he said this. I wanted to look into the rearview mirror and even sat straight up and tried to sneak a peek. I got taller than Abel sitting up this way.

"Well," the small man said.

"Well, what?" Abel asked.

"You guys like girls, and girls like rings." He flipped open the briefcase again and lifted the watches. Rows of rings, some with jewels, winked at us in the afternoon light. I picked up a tiny ring and asked, "How much for this one?"

"Eighty bucks."

"Eighty bucks!" I shoved it back into its velvety slot.

"Sixty-five."

"That's too much, sir," I said.

The man steered to the left to avoid a roadkill, a dog with a stiff leg in the air, and said, "Forty dollars. You're two tough cookies."

We told the man that we were college students and

between us we had only twenty-five dollars. He looked down at the briefcase and said, "The one with the zircon is twenty-five."

We told him again that we were on vacation and that we needed our money to get to Pismo Beach. At this, he closed the briefcase and remarked snidely, "And I thought you fellas liked girls."

We drove in silence for a while and then suddenly the small man braked and pulled to the shoulder of the road. "I have to take a left here. Sorry, fellas, I can't take you any farther."

We looked out the window at the rise of hills. The place was desolate.

While we gathered our stuff from the backseat, he got out and patted and adjusted his pillow. He got back in, waved good-bye, and roared off, his car kicking gravel at our legs. But instead of turning left as he had said, he continued up Highway 41.

"He's not turning," Abel shouted to me.

"He lied to us," I said, shocked that someone so puny could muster up a straight-faced lie.

We watched the car disappear in the distance. Things grew quiet. We turned in a circle looking at the roll of hills. Only after a black bird settled on the barbed-wire fence did Abel break the silence. "He had ugly rings anyhow."

We stood on the road, the wind whipping us with the dust and smells of the valley. Now and then a truck or car passed, and we stuck out our thumbs. But they roared past, slapping us with exhaust.

An hour passed, and then another. As dusk rose from the ground we realized that we would have to sleep on the side of the road. We hopped the barbed-wire fence and set up camp.

"I wish we were at the ocean," I complained. My hands were dirty, and my face, I could feel when I tried to smile, was coated with dust. And I was starting to get cold.

"We'll get there tomorrow," Abel said cheerfully. "This isn't so bad. *Míra,* we can see the mountains." I looked, but even though it was still light, all I could see was Abel's dirty face and miles of yellowish grass.

We cleared a space in the weeds, pulling at them until the earth, black as asphalt, became the floor we would sleep on. We washed our hands with water from our milk-carton canteen. We arranged our blankets and one sleeping bag. We thought about starting a small stick fire, but we decided it would attract the Highway Patrol or some mad farmer with a pitchfork. We said a prayer of thanks and opened a can of tuna, which we ate along with bread and pinches of barbecued potato chips. We drank our rationed water. For dessert we had a bag of doughnuts, which Glenda had tucked into Abel's shoulder bag.

It was soon dark, and we were shivering like wet dogs. The stars were silver, and the moon worked its way across the black sky. Abel and I talked about our mother and then our stepfather. We talked about girls we could have if we weren't so poor. I told him about Minerva, and Abel admitted that he still liked Glenda but knew he shouldn't get involved.

"Girls are strange," I lamented with a sigh. "I don't know what to say to them."

"I don't know what to say either," Abel admitted.

"I thought you did," I said with surprise.

It was completely dark. I couldn't tell if Abel was sitting, lying down, or standing up. He could have been standing on his head for all I knew.

"Nah, I don't know what to say to them. I don't even know if they like rings. Maybe that guy was lying to us."

We both agreed that the small man was a liar, and we both agreed that God would punish him in time. He could even now be on the side of the highway with a flat tire.

Then Abel asked quietly, "Do you ever think about Dad?"

"Yes," I whispered through my blanket.

"Do you miss him?"

"Yes, and Mom misses him, too," I said. "Abel, come on, no more."

We never talked about our father. He lived in our hearts and in the photograph of us on his shoulders at the beach in Santa Monica.

"Do you think Glenda thinks about her father?" I asked. "He's dead, too."

Abel shifted in his place, sighed, and then answered "Probably" after a long time of silence.

We slept some that night, but mostly we whimpered from the cold and the wind, and cursed the car that drove off without us in the direction of the crashing sea.

ten

the next morning we stuck our thumbs out for eight hours, dancing from foot to foot, while cars and trucks whizzed past, oblivious to our pleading glances. We spent another day on the side of the road, blinking dust and sunlight from our eyes. Toward evening, just after some teenagers in denim jackets threw eggs at us, one splattering my leg, we trudged off in different directions to cry—Abel toward a toppled water tank and me to a road sign with three bullet holes. Our tears didn't mean a thing to the dry earth.

We ate sandwiches and apples that night, our hands black with grime, and drank the last of our water. We shivered under a broad sky, talked about our failures, and dropped more tears into the dirt. Then, feeling better, I imagined an adventure where we didn't have to wear shoes, maybe in the Amazon jungle, and Abel imagined the sea air blowing through his hair and heart in Tahiti.

We finally got a ride the next morning and went as far as Kettleman City. We stopped at the public library, read the newspapers, and kicked around looking at storefronts. We spent most of our time in the city park and played softball with some kids whose gloves were too big for them. Happy once again, I brought out my colored pencils and paper, and drew the sea—plus a walrus that dripped sorrow from its large, round eyes.

"The ocean is just over there," Abel told me. He pointed in the direction of a hill that was mustering up shadows for the evening. "We almost made it, bro'."

I inhaled deeply but pulled in only the scent of a family barbecuing hot dogs. The sea was just too far away.

That evening, at the end of the third day of our spring vacation, we camped in the city park, and Abel suggested we return to Fresno. The way things looked, we might never get home if we didn't start back early enough. Mom and our teachers might begin to wonder what happened to us. So the next morning, after washing up at the gas station, we stuck our thumbs out and immediately got a ride back to Fresno with a preacher who gave off the scent of peach brandy. He kept his eyes more on us than on the road and had to brake and swerve more than once to avoid a collision. What I remember, aside from the stink of alcohol, was that he told us not to do what we really wanted to do, and then we would be able to do what was necessary. I chewed on this sliver of thought all the way to Fresno.

Since we never got a chance to see Pismo Beach, Abel and I were embarrassed. Now we were failures at hitch-hiking, and our friends might laugh at us. So we stayed in our apartment. We listened to the radio and scrubbed the bathroom until the ants and spiders didn't dare come out from behind the warped wallpaper. In case my class-mates asked what Pismo Beach looked like, I sketched a scene with boats docked at a pier.

We spent the rest of spring break chopping cotton, the blisters on our palms rising like pinkish moons. Glenda was working now. She came over only to play cards, and one evening her baby, the GI Joe in his mouth, kicked a sprinkler head again. It must have hurt because he dropped to the grass and drooled on the GI Joe slip-ping from the grip of his baby teeth. The next day when I saw the baby, his foot was bandaged with an old diaper.

Mom came to visit and gave me and Abel new Levi's and T-shirts and brought us a pile of tamales made by her *comadre*, Cuca. We ate them as soon as she left.

I felt good on Monday morning. Abel and I walked to school talking about what girls really liked to be called, aside from their names: "baby," "sweetie," "*mi ruca*," "honey," "*mi vida*," "sugar pie," "love," "darling." We talked about who should pay for dinner on a date, and if it was really proper for a guy to open a car door for a girl. We shrugged at the serious questions. *Some things can never be settled,* I thought. *Life is really a mystery after all.*

I was happy to sit, back straight, in Music Appreciation. I tapped my foot to Bach.

"You like this *música*?" Abel asked, a scowl on his face.

"*¡Simón!* It's cool," I said, head bouncing to the thump on the deep end of the keyboard. "Pretend the organ is really a guitar."

During break, I ran into Raul as he pulled the handle of a candy machine.

"Check it out," he yelled. He put his Snickers bar between his teeth like a bone and pulled out a news clipping, yellow and thin as a rose petal, a three-column article about the strike in Delano. I moved quickly through the words, thinking maybe the speed-reading class was paying off.

"That's cool," I said, returning it. "I'm proud of César Chávez."

"No, *ese! Mira!* Look close," Raul scolded. "That's me. The *vato* in the road."

I looked closely. It *was* Raul. It was his sombrero and huaraches, and it was his *bigote*. I was amazed. Maybe

Raul was really going places. He was only two years older than me, and already he was in the *Fresno Bee*.

"*¡Huelga!*" he howled as he put the news clipping back in his wallet. "Listen, man, you missed the meeting at Jesus's. We're holding a rally at the mall—tonight!" He pushed his index finger into my chest. "I want you to be there."

I didn't feel good after this. I saw Minerva, but I turned and hurried off, head down, wanting her, then not wanting her. I wondered if she would even go out with me if I asked. I sat on the lawn, cross-legged, and drew a walrus that looked more like a slug. I drew a shoelike boat caught between two waves.

That night Abel and I ate Top Ramen and fruit from the landlady's trees. Glenda came over with Larry, his feet tied in cloth bows, and brought four Popsicles. We sat on the lawn and played cards, mostly one-eyed Indian. After a while I told them that I had to go to a rally.

"*¿Dónde?*" Glenda asked.

"You speak Spanish, Glenda?" I asked, surprised.

"No, I just know that word and words like *adiós* and *enchilada*." She smoothed her baby's hair and said dreamily, "It would be really great if Larry could speak something different, like Persian or what people talk in Tibet."

Larry looked at us, his face red with Popsicle, and gargled, "Gaawaa."

Glenda clapped her hands on her lap and screamed with delight, "See, he's trying to communicate."

Larry gargled new words and then stabbed his ear with the Popsicle stick. Once again he went into one of those cries that takes a long time for the crying to start. Glenda picked him up and cooed in his good ear, "Oh, baby, too-too again."

I looked at Abel, who looked away, a tuft of grass in his hand.

"You want to come?" I asked Abel after the baby quieted down.

"*¿Dónde?*" he teased.

"Cut it out," I laughed. "You know where."

We all decided to go to the rally. But first Glenda ran to her apartment to take care of Larry. She returned shortly, his ear stuffed with balls of cotton. She called out, " 'Bye, Mom."

Mrs. Garoupa appeared at the screen door and waved with her fly swatter.

"Are you better?" Abel cooed, pinching Larry's dirty cheek.

The baby's eye leaked a tear. He turned away and hugged Glenda's neck.

We walked the four blocks to the downtown mall. The evening was warm. A neighbor, stripped to his waist, was watering the grass that ran along the curb. We smiled and waved, and when he lifted his arm to wave, I noticed a tattoo of a panther caught forever in a leap.

The mall was mostly empty, though music crackled from speakers. Two winos in crumpled hats were sitting near the fountain.

"I was in an antiwar rally once," Glenda said with a giggle, "but Mom got mad. She said I was acting like a hippie."

"You don't act like a hippie," Abel said. "You're like us."

"I know, but still."

We found the rally for the United Farm Workers on the north end of the mall, right in front of a closed store with whitewashed windows. There were lots of students and some priests and nuns, all chanting, "*¡El pueblo unido, jamás será vencido!*" The police were there, too, and a film crew from the local news. The crew had driven its van onto the sidewalk, and I wondered why the police didn't give them a ticket.

"Hey, look, it's Raul," I said as we cut across the mall.

Raul was circling the film crew, jabbing his finger at them.

"I bet you won't put this on TV, man," he scolded. "You don't have the *huevos*." He clutched his placard and scowled.

"We might," the crew leader in a blue baseball cap

muttered without interest as he uncoiled a loop of cable from around his ankle.

Raul circled a reporter like a rooster, his face busy with anger and sweat. "*¡Chale!* You never have our *gente, mi raza,* on TV. Just the *gavacho* president of the U.S. of A."

The reporter ignored him and signaled for one of the workers to move the sound equipment to the planter box, where the police were watching the crowd.

"*¿Entiendes?*" Raul shouted. "You get what I mean?"

"All right, we'll put you on." The reporter sighed and motioned with his hand for a guy to set up the camera and lights. He turned back to Raul and asked, "What is your name?"

Raul smiled. He looked at me and Abel, winked, and said in Spanish, "I'm going to tell the truth about America." To the reporter he said with pride, "Raul Salvador Garcia de la Peña."

The crowd was shouting "César *sí*, Reagan *no*," and the music of their voices was like a samba. When they saw that Raul was going to be interviewed, they shouted even louder.

"Hey, your mom gets to see you on TV," I said.

Raul's eyes became glassy at the thought.

The reporter played with his tie and looked up at the thick eye of the camera. He asked if his hair was OK, and Raul laughed and, clicking his tongue, asked, "*Pues,* Jesse, how do I look?"

"You look a little sweaty."

"That's 'cause I'm one of the people, bro'. We sweat for America. *¿Sabes?*"

The reporter smiled to the camera when a light went on. He became a different person. Looking like he was really worried about what was happening at the mall, he started, "We're down at the Fresno Mall, and we're speaking with—"

Raul cut him off. He stepped toward the camera and yelled, louder than necessary, in English, then Spanish, that the government was full of no-good *gavachos* and stupid pig cops, and if they didn't watch out, everything was going to change hands. Raul snapped his fingers and said, "Bombs will fall on you people! *¿Entiendes?* The *cholos* and *cholas* are gonna come down on you."

I glanced at the police, who were done fooling with Raul, I guess, because one of them jumped from the planter box and called him to come over. Raul told them to eat a truckload of cow pies. Just as Raul raised a clenched fist and shouted "*¡Viva la Raza!*" a nightstick caught him in the ear.

Blood spurted from Raul's head, scaring me so much that I took a step back.

"*Híjole,*" I whispered and crossed myself. "My Lord." Abel took Glenda's arm and led her away, the baby's head bouncing up and down with its own early load of memories.

One of the demonstrators jumped from the line and

pushed the cop. The cop, thick as a barrel, hardly moved, but his blue eyes were kind of wild and he looked like my stepfather when he couldn't find the screwdriver he needed. The cop swung again and missed. Raul scrambled to his feet and started running. I ran after him, asking if he was OK, if his ear hurt a lot. Raul was cussing under his breath and holding his ear. Blood oozed between his fingers and down his wrist.

We ran into Glenda and Abel at one end of the mall. They both looked scared, which made me scared. Abel put his arm around Raul and tried to calm him.

"I tol' you, *ese,*" Raul moaned as he straightened up and stared at the demonstrators who had run every which way.

Glenda dabbed at Raul's bloody wound with the cotton balls from the baby's ears, comforting him by saying that she had seen worse.

I ran away to cry with both hands over my ears.

eleven

raul had left a bloodstain on my new Levi's, and I wasn't sure if I should wear them on my date with Minerva. I had asked her out, and she had said yes.

"What do you think?" I asked Abel, who was working on a story about the Aztec calendar for his history class.

He examined the jeans, turning them over in his hands, and remarked, "Raul is pretty tough. Did you see his ear the next day? *¡Híjole!*"

"Come on, Abel," I whined. "Should I wear *these* or *these?*"

In my other hand I was holding a pair of green,

bell-bottom pants that had shrunk when I left them in the dryer for an hour. They were high-waters that yapped about my ankles, but I thought if I walked with my knees bent slightly Minerva wouldn't see they were too short.

"Don't worry, bro'," Abel said. "She won't notice the blood in the dark." He tossed me the jeans and returned to his work.

I dreaded the evening. I'd have to bathe long and hard, think of things to say, and spend my last five dollars. We were going to have a milkshake and take a walk on the levee near Sunnyside. I had arranged to borrow Glenda's Chevy, which I washed and cleaned. The car was a graveyard for GI Joes with their arms, heads, and legs pulled off, and the windows were a mess of fingerprints.

"I'll see you later," I told Abel after I had splashed my neck and face with Aqua Velva. I felt cool and clean, like a breath mint when you suck on it really hard. Abel went to the bedroom, where he fumbled in the drawer in the dark. He returned with a dollar and, patting my shoulder, said, "This is just in case."

"Thanks," I mumbled. It made me sad that my brother liked me so much.

I drove to Minerva's small house near the fairgrounds, on a street with cars parked on the lawns. A row of rusty coffee cans with sticklike plants lined the front porch. A porch light glowed with a halo of orange haze, and a large swamp cooler sat in the window, leaking water. A cat was dozing on the cooler. When he looked at me, eyes blinking sleepily, I saw that one of his fangs was sticking straight out like a toothpick.

"Here goes," I sighed, and rapped a knuckle lightly on the glass door. I heard footsteps, and the radio's volume went down to a buzz of violins and bleating trumpets. Minerva unlatched the chain and swung open the door. "Hi, Jesse." She peered over my shoulder and asked, "Is that your car?"

In the dark, Glenda's Chevy didn't look that bad, just long. I smiled and said, "Yeah."

Minerva walked me to a back room and introduced me to her father, who pulled his eyes away from the television and extended his hand. When I shook it, I could feel the years of work. I could see in his lined face that he had stared over a continent of cotton plants, beets, and vineyards. "*Mucho gusto, señor,*" I said, trying to sound respectful. He nodded at me, and Minerva introduced me to her mother, who had come into the room. She was small and seemed kind. I could feel my Aqua Velva losing some of its strength. Just what were they planning? I wondered.

"You're in college?" Minerva's mother asked in Spanish as she prodded us from the den to the kitchen, where Mexican music whispered from the radio on the counter.

"Yes," I answered in English. "I'm studying art. I want to paint."

"*Qué bueno,*" she said. "Is your family from here?"

"*Sí,*" I answered. I eyed the portraits of Jesus and John F. Kennedy on the walls. "But my father is dead."

"Oh, how sad," she said in English, and her smile sank into a gray line. She thought about this piece of information and then said, "I don't want Minerva to come home too late. Use your judgment, *mi'jo.*"

I looked down at Minerva's mom's hand resting on my arm like a sparrow. I assured her that we would be home by ten-thirty, eleven at the latest.

We left the house, Minerva touching my shoulder. Her hand was more like a dove than a sparrow, and in a moment I saw how time can change a person.

I opened the car door for Minerva and saw her immediately take in the smell of another woman. She wet her lips and looked at me suspiciously.

"Do you have a girlfriend?" she asked as I pulled the car from the curb. "I promise, I won't get mad."

"No," I said as I maneuvered the Chevy around the block to Ventura Boulevard and headed toward First Street. "The car doesn't really belong to me. It belongs to Glenda."

"Who's Glenda?"

"A girl on our street. She's not married, but she's got this baby."

Minerva didn't say anything for a while. We headed north to Carnation Dairy, the car squeaking over each hole. Then she asked as we idled at a red light, "Are you lying, Jesse? I want to know."

"Minerva," I said. "Be cool. I don't have a girl."

With this she smiled and moved close to me. She placed her dovelike hand on my sleeve and fixed a kind of romantic gaze on me. Her eyes were large and clear as a cat's, and I could smell her perfume and hair spray. She looked nice, teeth milky white and almost perfect.

"But don't you have a boyfriend?" I reminded her. By now my Aqua Velva was nearly gone and I was smelling more like a boy than a date. I peered down at the bloodstain on my jeans and covered it with my right hand.

"He's not really my boyfriend, Jesse. He's just a guy that I see now and then. We hardly kiss or anything."

At Carnation Dairy we ordered milkshakes and a plate of fries. Minerva sipped her shake and ate some fries dipped in ketchup. I sucked on my chocolate shake, my cheeks going hollow on a real hard blast. I told Minerva that one day I would like to go to Paris.

"Why? Don't you like Fresno?"

"Yeah, but you know, I'd like to travel."

Minerva thought about this for a moment and said she would like to go to Santa Cruz. She had a girlfriend there who was a nurse's aide at the county hospital. She had just gotten married and was having a baby in July.

I didn't know what to say. I took another blast of my milkshake and pitched two french fries into my mouth. I liked the mixture of sweet and salty. I pointed with my fork and said, "You see how there are no Mexicans here. Just *gavachos.*"

Minerva turned her head left and right and then caught an image of herself in the window. She stared at herself for a second and then said, "That's 'cause they don't know how to work. If they did, they'd be here."

The bill came to only $3.45, plus thirty-five cents tip. I paid and we left, Minerva touching my arm. We drove to the levee, where we parked the car and listened to the radio play "A Hard Day's Night."

"Do you really want to be an artist?" Minerva asked in the dark. She was twisting a ring on her finger. Her eyes were eager for something to happen. I thought of putting my arms around her.

"Yeah, I do. I want to work in oils eventually, but I have to work in pencils now because it's cheaper. First, of course, I want to travel."

"Come on, Jesse, stay in Fresno. You're going to get lost if you go to Paris."

"No, me and Abel want to travel. You learn more."

Minerva snuggled up to me, a fingernail clicking on the buttons of my shirt. I could smell her perfume, hair spray, and french fries. "You're cute, Jesse."

I looked down at my lap. I didn't know what to say, except "I guess so."

She laughed and buried a kiss on my throat, and before I knew it, she was kissing me real hard, her tongue like a lizard darting in and out of my mouth. I liked it but I was scared. I pushed her away.

"What's wrong, Jesse?" she asked. "Don't you like me?"

"Sure I do." I looked out the window and said, "Hey, let's go for a walk by the river."

"That's not a river, it's a ditch!"

"You know what I mean. Come on."

Minerva pouted but opened her door. She went with me, an arm around my arm, as we walked along the levee. We stared at the water. I saw a tire float by, cracking the moonlight on the surface of the water. We stopped, hugged, and once again her tongue flickered in my mouth. She said she liked me, and I told her I liked her, too. Then her tongue went to town. One of her breasts poked my heart, and it didn't even hurt. But all this kissing stopped when a carload of drunk guys came by. One of the car's headlights was out, and they must have been out of beer because they screamed and asked if we had a six-pack. They tooted the horn and got out, staggering.

"No, we don't have anything to drink," I yelled, trying to sound cheerful. But I was worried. They yelled and cussed and approached us, clutching beer bottles. Minerva huddled at my side.

"What do you know, it's Romeo and Juliet," one of

them sneered. He was weaving drunkenly in his cowboy boots.

"Come on," I whispered to Minerva as I prodded her to the car. One of the guys stopped me. His hand felt like a claw on my shoulder. We recognized each other; we were from the same high school.

I thought maybe our school pride would bring us together, and we would laugh and slap each other on the shoulder. He would ask about Minerva and apologize, and then he'd ask me what I was up to these days. But none of this happened. He threw his empty beer bottle into the ditch and grabbed me around the throat. He said I smelled like a sissy; he must have picked up on what was left of my Aqua Velva.

"I never liked your ugly mug, you and your brother, what's-his-name," he snarled. He hit me in the face, and I stagger-stepped backward holding my nose. I could feel the warm blood curl from between my fingers. He was huge, especially in his cowboy boots, and his two friends were even bigger. I stood there, holding my nose, pretending that I was hurt worse than I was. I dropped to one knee and pulled my fingers away. Blood dripped into the dirt when I shook my head up and down.

"You sissy," he growled, his boots kicking gravel as he staggered toward their car. "You and me went to the same school, and you can't even fight." He unzipped his pants and peed on his own tire, sighing. They got in their car and sped away with both headlights off.

Minerva ran to the car and cried into the twin doves of her hands. I followed her slowly, got into the car, started it up, and drove off. She hardly looked at me as I drove her home, steering with one hand and holding my nose with the other.

"I'm sorry you had to see that," I told Minerva.

"How's your nose?" she asked, peeking from behind her hands.

"I think it's OK." I sucked in and, trying to be funny, told her that I could smell the burgers frying at the A&W Root Beer on Tulare. She cried even more.

When I dropped her off I thought about telling her that the evening had been pretty nice, except for the last part. I thought about kissing her, but I guessed it wasn't the right time. My face was smeared with blood.

Abel was upset when I got home and thought of calling our cousin Lalo, who was so mean he had L-O-V-E and H-A-T-E cut into his knuckles. The white boys wouldn't stand a chance. They'd find themselves floating with the tires in the ditch.

"We'll get them," Abel yelled, his fists curled at his sides. He paced the living room.

"It doesn't hurt that much," I said from the couch. "Just when I laugh." I laughed, and blood oozed from both nostrils and some trickled down my throat.

Abel calmed down after a while and asked how my date was. I told him it was OK and got up, fished into my pants, and handed him his dollar back. "We had milkshakes and fries." Behind my bloody face I beamed and said, "Minerva kisses really hard."

Abel's eyes brightened, and then he said thoughtfully, "Love comes with a price, bro'."

My new jeans, soaking in the bathtub, now had two bloodstains—Raul's and mine.

twelve

the next morning I wore an orange shirt with long sleeves and my green bell-bottom pants. Though tender to the touch, my nose was functioning again. I could smell Abel cooking *huevos con* weenies for burritos, a weekday treat that was steaming up the kitchen window. I looked at the frying pan. The weenies, sliced into circles, were jumping up and down like little troopers, the burner turned up all the way. While Abel cooked I checked my new Levi's. I wrung them out, scratched at the bloodstains, and hung them on the back fence.

"This is good," I said to Abel, who was eating standing over the cold floor furnace. He blew on his burrito and said, "I hate getting hit in the nose."

"Me, too," I agreed. "It makes your eyes water."

But I wasn't feeling too bad. Love has a big price, as Abel had said beautifully. In bed I had prayed, and that made me feel good. I promised God that I would return to a deeper faith and that I would try to forgive Ron Dryer, whose name had come back to me while I prayed. I forgave him and forgave his friends for laughing at me.

After breakfast we hurried to class. I wouldn't have to see Minerva because my biology teacher had arranged a field trip to the country, where we were going to take sweep samples of insects and ask farmers questions about what it's like to farm.

We were to meet in the parking lot by the library and caravan by car. Instead of his usual gray suit, my biology teacher wore baggy khakis and a plaid shirt. In the cool morning his breath floated on the air. He was holding a clipboard to his chest, and when students approached, he asked our names and then, with a quick flick, checked them off.

Only half the class showed up, and the teacher sent someone to see if the others were in the classroom. Ten minutes later the student came back with eight others who thought we were supposed to meet at the classroom.

I got in the backseat of the biology teacher's car, a station wagon with a litter of burger wrappers on the floor. He apologized for the mess. He told us he had six kids, including one who had already flunked out of college.

The tires whined on the road. Wind whistled through the wing window and diesel trucks whizzed by, rocking our car. I was saved from boredom by the landscape, which I recognized from days chopping cotton and picking grapes. It kicked in a dusty memory of the time I worked on my knees nine hours—one hundred seventy-eight trays of grapes—so I could buy my mom an umbrella, one I had spotted hanging from the limp arm of a mannequin in a window. I sweated gobs for that umbrella, and when Mom unwrapped it at Christmas, she cried, "And I thought it was an ironing board!" She jabbed it in the air like a spear and said, "I hope it rains." But there was always more sweat than rain.

Gazing out the back window I could see the faces of the students directly behind us. They were laughing and enjoying themselves. Maybe they were even singing, because their mouths seemed more open than usual.

We drove thirty miles. When we pulled over to the side of the road, gravel crunching beneath the tires, I was amazed because it was the spot where Abel and I had gotten stuck hitchhiking to Pismo Beach. I got out of the car, stunned. This was the exact place. I turned to the field where we had cleared a place to sleep.

"Man," I said under my breath.

The other cars pulled over to the side of the road, and the students piled out and picked up butterfly nets. I walked away for a moment. I had the feeling that God had arranged all this, that I had to reexamine this place. A blade of clouds sliced across the sky. Two black birds honked grotesquely from a barbed-wire fence.

When I went to get a butterfly net, there was only one left, and the net was more like a knot of string than a thing to capture insects. I took it and joined the others in the field. They were batting the air for insects, laughing because it was fun and nothing like Biology.

I walked over to where Abel and I had slept. The grass was growing back, covering up the evidence that we had camped our loneliness there. I raked back the grass and discovered two apple cores, whittled down to brown rot by red ants. I remembered when Abel and I had eaten those apples. It had been dark, and neither of us could see the other's jaws going up and down on the sweetness of apple. We shivered that night and tried to convince each other that it was a learning experience to sleep in a field within earshot of a highway. We told stories, too, but mostly we just sat, cross-legged under the huge weight of stars and the push of time.

My eyes filled with tears. I thought of my brother, and I thought of my stepfather, who was probably scrubbing a piece of furniture with a wad of steel wool, his knuckles a nest of wiry fibers. I thought of Mom with a telephone to her ear, and my dead father on his rack of blackness, lighting up the earth with the glow of his bones. Everything moves, including the dead, and I knew that God wanted me to return and look at where I had slept on the damp ground, there, where a gopher poked its slick head through the crumbly earth. I promised that I would go to five o'clock mass when I returned.

I rubbed the tears from my eyes and followed the others up the hill, swiping at the spring air. The whistling sound of flying nets cut through the air, that and laughter, where an hour ago had been only silence.

Our teacher kept up with us awhile, explaining that we would collect insects today and examine them later on our own. We were to compare them with the insects in our biology book. He pointed out some rock formations and made us hush when he thought he had spied a fox. But the fox was only a bun-round boulder poking through the grass.

By noon I had collected three powdery butterflies and a squat bottle. I turned the bottle over in my hand and wondered who had drunk from it. They were gone, their faces pressed in some photo album sitting in a trunk in any of a thousand barns in the valley. It was scary knowing that one day no one would know who you were or that you stood knee-deep in grass.

We stayed for three hours before the teacher waved for us to come back. His knees were wet from kneeling on the ground and his hair was blown into a mess. His bald spot shone in the sunlight. Instead of going with the teacher on the return trip, I climbed in the back of a pickup, my knees curled to my chest. The wind sucked around me, fluttering my clothes and hair.

That evening, on the way to mass at St. John's, I changed into my really old jeans and paisley long-sleeved shirt. I was choking on sadness. I walked past the courthouse where the Armenian men played dominoes and checkers, and squirrels made their grimy living on litter and the droppings from trees. I got to one knee, snapping my fingers. I beckoned the squirrels, but they just stared at me.

I was the only young person at five o'clock mass. Most of the others were old women with frayed bandannas tied over their hair. Their shoulders were hunched from sorrow or from the weight of work, marriage, and armfuls of babies.

I listened to the priest, whose eyes were smoky with belief. He coughed in the middle of a prayer and spoke softly about the Host as salvation. I always felt lost when it came to things like the Trinity, original sin, and the Assumption of Mary. Once, when I was eleven and jiggling a free Coke from a machine outside the parish house, I overheard the priests and nuns bickering about "infallibility." Their argument astonished me. I had never had the courage to question the catechism—Why do we need God's revelation? Does God change? How many angels are there? When is war just?

I had gone to Catholic school for three years, from first through third grades, and although I prayed on my knees in my bedroom, religion was my worst subject, even worse than math. I was afraid that God might not appreciate my sorrow. I worried that if I didn't learn my prayers, if I couldn't answer on my own "Why does God love you?" I would not be saved but would be swept away with the multitudes. My faith was strong, but my understanding was weak.

After mass I circled the garden on the side of the church, where a fountain splashed water from a concrete urn into a mossy pond. I discovered three fish, their gills opening and closing like wounds. I ran my fingers under the water and crossed myself. I thought of Minerva, who was probably copying her homework from a history book. I wondered if she was wondering about me. I knew that she liked me. She had been scared for herself but embarrassed for me when Ron Dryer had punched me. Her mother wanted me to like her, but her father, hurt from years of work, was just glad to sit down in a chair and watch others wrestle through adventures on television.

I checked the Coke machine, running a finger in the slot where the change falls. I opened the door of the machine and pulled on one of the icy Cokes. The Coke wouldn't give, a good sign, I thought. If it had, I would have sinned. I would have had to pay it back by some misfortune—a wind picking up and slapping dirt into my good eye. I smiled, turned, and started back to the apartment.

thirteen

the sun flared behind a torn billboard and was almost gone when I returned to the apartment. Glenda's Chevy was not in front. I passed Mrs. Garoupa's apartment, where June bugs were sucking on the screen door, a meager living even for a lowly insect. I could see Mrs. Garoupa plopped on the couch in front of her TV, a pinwheel of colored light in her face, a rolled-up newspaper in her hands.

Abel and Leslie were sitting on the steps of the porch, munching on orange slices, their fingers wet with juice.

"Hi, Leslie," I said. "Hey, Abel. Did Mom give us anything?"

Wednesday was usually the day Mom came by with a gift of tortillas, a can of soup or tuna, soap, or a dollar bill in an old PG&E envelope. Abel shook his head no.

Leslie held up an orange for me. I took it and rolled it between my palms. It always amazed me. Oranges were a winter fruit, but they hung on, bitter in April, for free picking. I tore into the orange with my fingers and began to eat.

"Leslie's gonna store some artwork in the shed," Abel explained. "It's too big to fit in his car. Mrs. Garoupa doesn't mind."

"What are you working on?" I asked.

Leslie was a good artist. He was far better than me or even the teacher, Mr. Helperin, who seemed to like scenes that didn't mean much to the rest of us. It seemed we hadn't learned much from him, except that we should try our best and never store oil paints by the heater.

The three of us went to the garage. Leslie wiped his hands on his jeans and unrolled a large canvas over an old wringer washer. Abel pulled the chain of the overhead light, and the canvas shone in the glare. It was a painting of three large-eyed monkeys frolicking in a banana tree.

"That's us—*changos!*" Abel joked after a moment of study.

Leslie laughed at this, and I had to smile because the three monkeys, cheeks fat with orange pulp, it seemed, were looking right at us. They were our cousins from some not-so-distant past when we'd been leaping over alligators and bubbling quicksand.

"I'm going to enter it in the art exhibit next week. Jesse, you should do something, too."

"*Chale,*" I said. "No way."

"Come on, man," Abel begged. "You're good. You got that horse you keep drawing."

"That's just practice drawing, Abel."

"Try something new," Leslie encouraged.

I stared at the three monkeys and then at Abel and Leslie. We rolled up the canvas, pulled the chain, and headed back to the apartment. Leslie said, "I heard you got in a fight."

"Yeah, some guy socked me in the nose." I touched my nose, which was still tender. I was scared to sneeze.

"Too bad," Leslie said flatly. "If you want, I can even the score."

"Nah, it was just a misunderstanding." I glanced down at my stained jeans. "They were brand new a couple of days ago. First Raul bled on them, and then I did."

"*Qué lástima,*" Leslie said with a pretty good accent.

Leslie had brought over eggs and bologna. We cooked up a storm, the quartered bologna flapping like tongues in a black frying pan. We added bell peppers and made toast. Smoke filled the kitchen. Steam dripped from the kitchen window over the sink. I wiped the window and looked out; Glenda was parking her Chevy.

"Let's invite Glenda," I called out. I was feeling happy because we seemed like one family.

Leslie perked up. Although Abel had cooled on her, Leslie was beginning to like her a lot. During art studio, while he dotted a canvas with really nice Seurat-like specks, he had mentioned her to me several times—was she really single? Was that huge person, Mrs. Garoupa, her mother? Did she like the Beatles or the Stones better?

He broke another egg, and I raced to the front door to invite Glenda. The baby was in her arms, a small bandage on his forehead, a new injury for the close of yet another day. He was pouting.

"Glenda, do you want to have dinner with us?" I asked. "Leslie's here."

"I'll be there in a sec," she said with a smile, and hurried into her apartment.

It was like a party that night. Glenda brought us a rug, which she had gotten from Goodwill. And she brought over a carton of Neapolitan ice cream, mine and Abel's favorite.

I started my speed-reading homework while Leslie and Glenda were still there. I tried to explain speed-reading. You have to pick out key words and forget the rest.

"I don't understand how," Leslie said, lifting his eyebrows to Glenda. "You think it works?"

"Sure," Glenda said. "It's a science."

"I'm not sure myself," I admitted.

"Show us how it works," Abel mumbled with a spoon in his mouth. He tossed me his history book. "Here."

I took the book, weighed it in my hands, and thumbed through it until I found some easy pages about the Civil War. I told Leslie, "Count to a minute when I say." The three of them looked at me, serious, because they had never seen anyone speed-read before. I sucked in a lungful of air. I looked down at the page and shouted, "Go." My eyes buzzed and rattled over the dense pages. I picked up references to cannonballs, Lincoln not liking South Carolina, General Sherman, a dead horse, railroad tracks torn up, fife music on both sides, the Mississippi River, death by the thousands. . . . My eyes had hit the word *submarine* when Leslie called, "Time."

I looked up, a mustache of sweat on my lip. My eyes hurt from pulling right to left, right to left at a great speed. But I seemed none the wiser. I was confused and dizzy.

"OK, what happened? What did you read?" Abel asked.

I told him it was about death and destruction and the country twisted over big issues. I slapped the book closed and mumbled mournfully, "See, I'm not so sure it works."

They slapped their thighs and laughed. They stopped

laughing when I got up, went to the bedroom, and returned with a sheet of waxed paper. The three butterflies were like crumbs—their antennas were broken, their legs pulled in, and their wings folded like rags.

"Oh, how sad," Glenda lamented.

I told them about the biology field trip and wanted to tell Abel that I had collected them from the field where he and I slept. But I held my tongue. I told them instead that I had to study them but was really too sad to turn them over with a pair of tweezers and explain their meaning in a simple, double-spaced paragraph.

Leslie slept on our floor that night, right on the new carpet, and the next day we got a ride to school with him. I knew that Minerva didn't have any Tuesday-Thursday classes, but I watched out for her anyway. I still wasn't prepared to talk with her, to ask how she felt watching me get beat up.

As I hurried across the scraggly grass, I spied Raul's face on the front cover of the school newspaper. I peeled a newspaper from the rack. I was surprised that you could get hit in the ear and the next week have a story written about it. Raul was the bravest person I knew, next to Leslie, who had been in Vietnam and had had to hug himself against gunfire.

In the art studio I worked on a watercolor of picketing workers marching along a vineyard. It was a row of workers, one taller than the next, all pushed together, all with sad but determined faces. I liked what I was creating with the pinks and blacks and got a tingling feeling in my shoulders, a sign that I was on the right track.

Some of the other students were just talking by the open window, pulling on the cord of the blinds so that the light flickered. Some were working on homework for other classes. Only a few were taking our two hours together seriously.

Leslie came over to see my progress. He didn't say anything, just sat next to me and whittled a pencil, the flakes falling like snow to the floor. After a while he touched my shoulder and said quietly, "You have a good brother."

I nodded and smiled.

Then he asked, "Do you think your brother still likes Glenda?"

I stopped painting and turned and faced Leslie. He looked too tall for the chair he was sitting in and scared of my answer. I looked at his hurt eye. "No," I said softly. "I think it's OK to like her, Leslie."

He chuckled at this and remarked after a moment of thought, "OK, I think I will." He got up and left, and Mr. Helperin, our teacher, came over to look at my painting. He fiddled for a mint in his shop coat and said, "Jesse, you're improving."

He bit into his breath mint, hard, and when he said, "You're doing a good job," I could smell the coolness of his words.

fourteen

days later, when I returned from school, Leslie and Glenda were together on Mrs. Garoupa's front porch, and Larry was playing in the flower bed. The garden hose was set before him, and water rose over his pudgy legs, and he dripped a fistful of mud onto the water's mirrory surface. While he squealed and splashed about, I thought of God shaping us from mud, stuff good in itself but useless when thrown about by a baby with three teeth.

Having forgotten Glenda, Abel was now talking about a girl in his history class. He'd tell me about her freckles and her nose, remembering in detail how she poked her soda with a straw. He told me she had a VW and nice clothes, and he regretted getting his tattoo— that bluish cross riding the flap of skin between his thumb and index finger.

Minerva had ignored me ever since our date to Carnation Dairy. In Western Civ, I smiled at her and she smiled back, mouth closed. I guessed that meant she wanted to be just acquaintances instead of friends. So I spent my free time at school leaning against a eucalyptus, the rush of wind peeling at sheets of bark. I thought about Lupe again, and wondered if she ever thought about me.

It was the last month of the spring semester, and Abel and I were getting Cs, not Bs, in Music Appreciation. We planned to attend a free concert of chamber music for extra credit. Abel invited Maureen, the girl he liked, and she picked us up in her VW. Abel smelled like Aqua Velva.

Abel introduced me on the front steps of our porch. "This is my brother," he said, his face huge from smiling.

I shook Maureen's hand, which was pink and cool, and she gave off a sweet scent, too. Abel and I piled into the car, with me in the back. My poor brother breathed in Maureen's beauty all the way to the Lutheran church where the concert was held.

"Do you think we should go in?" I asked Abel in the parking lot.

"Why not?"

I was staring at the church with its simple cross. "It's not Catholic. I'm not sure if we're supposed to."

"Jesse, wise up," Abel groaned.

"But you know what Father Moreno says."

He gave me a push and said I should realize by now that it was OK to go places that were non-Catholic. I looked down at my shoes, hurt that my brother would tell me to wise up in front of a girl I didn't know. I told Abel and Maureen I wanted to stay outside as long as I could because it was a warm night.

"Suit yourself!" Abel snapped, which hurt me even further.

I stayed outside for a while, and I walked around to the back of the church, where two musicians dressed in tuxedos were smoking cigarettes. When someone called they tossed the cigarettes to the ground and smashed them with the heels of their shoes, which even in the half-light were shiny as mirrors. A cough of smoke rose into the air, and they were gone.

Back at the front of the church I went in, crossing myself in memory of our Lord. The church was crowded, the air moist with talk and lots of bodies pressed together. Abel and Maureen had saved a place for me. Abel even patted the chair.

"It's hot," I said, sitting down.

The musicians were already seated. They looked out at the audience, and we looked at them. The conductor came out to a flurry of applause. He looked so happy that I applauded hard and then stood up to pull some notepaper from my back pocket. He bowed, turned to his little orchestra, raised his baton, and then, his head jerking a little bit, the music started.

I turned to Abel and whispered, "You got a pencil?"

Abel, making a face, handed over a dull pencil with a nibbled eraser. I figured that I had better take notes so that later I could assemble my thoughts.

For twenty minutes the violin was kind of nice, but the song droned on until my eyes watered. Abel's eyes watered, too, and three times I had to force back a wet yawn. I looked around at the people in the audience, their faces bursting with sweat, and I thought that maybe some music was just no good.

We stayed for only half of the concert—we felt we'd heard enough. We drove to an A&W for a root beer, a sludge of ice on our mugs slowly letting loose and crumbling onto the Formica table. Maureen told us a little about herself, how she had moved from Bakersfield to Fresno when she was eight. She cleared her throat with a swig of root beer and dipped a finger in a puddle of melted ice. She told us her father sold orthopedic limbs, legs and hands. I looked down at my own hands, a slant of pale hairs on each knuckle, and was grateful that I could lift my mug to my mouth without difficulty. She said her mother worked part-time at a dress shop.

When we got home Abel and I busied ourselves writing a paper for music appreciation class. We described the music repeatedly as beautiful and the instruments as fine examples of modern craftsmanship. The musicians were talented, we wrote, and unique people in a unique time. We hoped this kind of critique would pull us from a C to a B.

Maureen was my brother's girlfriend now. I was sad that he wanted to be with her and not me. To keep my mind busy for the remaining weeks of school, I decided to join MEChA. Raul had been pestering me, so one night while Leslie was with Glenda, Abel with Maureen, and Mrs. Garoupa with the baby, a new bandage on his elbow, I walked to a meeting at Jesus's house on San Pablo Avenue. Jesus, an older guy and a Vietnam vet like Leslie, was cool. He let the *Mechistas* hang out at his apartment, which was upstairs over a garage, and sometimes even bought them beer if they promised not to drink too much and fall out the windows. But mostly he just sat in the background, chuckling and feeling good that so many brown people were in his house.

"*¡Órale!*" Raul shouted when he made out my scrubbed face in the early dark. He was hanging out the window, admiring the sunset with a really nice-looking Chicana. "It's my *carnal,* Jesse. Where you been, brother? Hitting *los libros o qué?*"

I nodded, called out, "Knock-knock," and entered. I was in a small kitchen, with plastic beads swishing in the doorway. Over the refrigerator hung portraits of Che Guevara, Pancho Villa, and César Chávez during his forty-day hunger strike. A Porky Pig cookie jar stood on the counter, and a palm leaf twisted into a cross hung on the cupboard.

Jesus was stirring a batch of grape Kool-Aid, the ice cubes clanging against the sides of the aluminum pitcher. A woman, his girlfriend, I figured, was at the stove popping popcorn. When she wiggled the pot over the burner, her hips moved in a *cha-cha-cha*. Her mouth was a bud of glossy red.

I introduced myself to Jesus and the woman, whose name was Yolanda, and carried the popcorn over to the coffee table in the living room. A few of the *Mechistas* were looking at magazines or talking about school. They smiled at me, a good sign, because I wanted to feel wanted. I took a seat on a small green hassock.

That night we debated the issues of Nixon and Vietnam. Raul had brought a small tape recorder and wanted to see what we sounded like when we talked politics.

"I'll go first," Raul said, licking his buttery fingers. He took a swig of Kool-Aid and said, "That stupid Nixon. I'm going to thrash the *cabrón* if I ever see him walking in *mi barrio*."

"*Pues,* how you going to know?" someone asked. "How you gonna know when he's in Fresno?"

Everyone turned to Raul for an answer.

"Miracles happen, bro'. It's a miracle that we're in Jesus's home, *¿Qué no?* I mean, I might run into the dude and then again I might not. I'm just saying that if I *do,*

I'm going to throw some *chingadasos* on his ugly *cara.*
¿Sabes?"

"What about the Secret Service, man?" someone
asked.

"*Pues,* the Secret Service ain't nothing but *gavachos*
in sunglasses!"

Raul's eyes flashed with anger at the possibility of
Nixon daring to enter his barrio without his say-so. Raul
looked around the room in a threatening way, and once
he felt he had captured everyone's attention said, "OK,
I'm done. Who's next?"

We went around the room, and some voiced how
they felt about Nixon. All of us were angry. We said that
Nixon looked like a crook, which sent the conversation
in a different direction. We began to debate whether
what we look like is what we are.

"*Chale,*" Jesus said in a cool whisper. "How can you
say you are what you look like? Say if some *vato* is not
attractive, say he's *feo.* Does that give you permission to
say that person is ugly inside? *¿Sabes?*"

This got a lot of attention, and we continued our
debate, the tape recorder picking up our words. We
talked about Chicanos in Vietnam. Jesus was the au-
thority, and he reported that the *carnales* were falling,
shedding real blood while the white boys were checking
it out with binoculars and road maps. It made me sad
that Mexican people were doing all the fighting just the
way we were doing all the farmwork.

"We never get to check things out," Jesus said, his hands curled into binoculars and scanning the living room. He said, "I see you, and you, and you," stopping on each of our faces. "And I see you," he said to me. "How old are you, dude?" he asked me, lowering his arms.

"Eighteen," I lied. I licked my lips and lowered my gaze, ribbons of sweat running from under my arms. The Mechistas, I could feel, were staring at me.

"*Pues, su tío* Samuel is gonna look you up. Did you get a letter yet?"

He meant my draft letter, which I would get when I turned eighteen. Abel had gotten his first letter with his draft number on it the year before, and I knew what they looked like. He was due to get another letter.

"No, I just got a letter from the marines." I looked around the room and said bravely, "I tore it up."

"Marines! They're the worst," Jesus scolded. "When your draft letter—the real one—comes, just write RETURN TO SENDER, and drop it in the box, *ese*."

We talked about an hour, and then Raul played back the tape. At first I heard the slurping of Kool-Aid and then Raul, who sounded far away. His words began to slur, as the tape recorder trudged along on feeble power.

"*Ay, chihauhua,*" Raul yelled, shaking the tape recorder. "Stupid batteries!"

He clicked his tongue, shrugged his shoulders and muttered under his breath, "*¡No importa!*" He and the nice-looking Chicana stuck their heads out the window, and he pointed to the moon, then to a streetlight. He said something about the expanding universe. I turned away and helped clean up the living room. I thanked Jesus and Yolanda for having me over and waved goodbye to Raul and his girl. I hurried away as fast as I could, jumping a fence into an alley busy with barking dogs and fence-walking cats. Instead of going home I walked to Lupe's house and stood there for a while. I chewed a thumbnail with my nervous teeth and left with the taste of blood in my mouth, my hunger having gone too far.

fifteen

mom worked the car back and forth into a space near the college library, her brow pleated with worry. When she couldn't get it right, even though she was sitting on two pillows and had the help of students walking past, we traded places. I went back and forth as well, but not so many times.

It was May. Swamp coolers and air-conditioners were being put to the test. For a week the early summer heat had pressed us into our houses or the nearest shadows. Dogs lay their barking to rest and cats blinked from behind forts of yellow grass.

I had kept out of the heat, too. I was writing term

papers, listening to music, and watching my brother fall in love with Maureen. She would come over at night to see Abel, and, with Leslie and Glenda, they would sit on the lawn and talk about traveling. Abel was interested in going to Egypt. When I told Abel that it was hotter there than in Fresno, he told me that I didn't get his point, that heat had nothing to do with where he wanted to go.

I decided to enter the art exhibit at school. I had worked and reworked my drawing of the United Farm Workers picketing in Delano until I thought I had finally got their sadness right. It had to do with how they stood, their bodies leaning slightly forward so that they looked like they were walking into wind. Leslie helped. He had moved into the shed and no longer slept in his car. He would sit with me in the afternoon, sketching and humming in a way that made me feel at peace. Abel was now working at Maureen's dad's office assembling plastic fingers and even painting the knuckles with nests of fake hairs.

I had invited Mom to see my artwork hanging in the exhibit. She had taken off early from work, a loss of $9.50. "But what the heck," she said cheerfully as she drove to the college with both hands on the steering wheel and the turn signal blinking left.

The exhibition was in the cafeteria. While we walked in that direction, I pointed out the library, the music hall, the administration building, the commons. Mom nodded at each building but only stopped to examine a leaf from a flowering bush. Looking around, she broke it off and then asked me to go to the men's room and bring back a wet paper towel. I did. When I returned Mom had snipped off some more plants, a whole handful, and was talking with the gardener in Spanish. I waited in the shade, holding the paper towel, for Mom to stop chatting.

We arrived at the cafeteria early. The janitor was mopping a corner of the floor, and a woman was arranging plates of carrot sticks and radishes on a table covered with butcher paper. We entered anyway. The American and California flags were limp as pants pockets turned inside out. Mr. Helperin was standing among some students, all with long hair and tie-dyed shirts.

"Is this where you eat, *mi'jo*?" Mom asked as she looked around, her nose quivering.

"I bring my lunch, Mom."

Mom walked slowly, looking around, her purse on her arm. She stared at some artwork for a long time before she asked, "Is it broken?"

"What?"

"That! *Mira!*"

She was pointing to a mobile of our congressmen with their eyes jabbed out. I had watched Leo, the artist, cut and paste pictures in class. He threaded faces of fifty congressmen on string, clapped his hands free of paste and dust, and stood back to admire his work. I wasn't sure if it was art, but Mr. Helperin admired what he was doing, even helped Leo find pictures of the congressmen. Leo said it represented a blind congress. Can't they see the war is wrong? he had asked in class. He had let the mobile blow in the breeze from a fan to cool the congressmen's aggression.

We walked toward the mobile, and standing almost directly beneath it, Mom turned each face over like a price tag. Finally, she asked, "¿*Qué pasó?* Who are they?"

"Politicians," I answered.

"How come their faces are up there?"

"It's art, Mom."

Mom looked at me and said, "No."

"It *is*, Mom."

She shook her head and looked through her purse for a piece of Juicy Fruit. She tore it in half and gave me the bigger of the two pieces. We then approached a pair of boxing gloves with their guts ripped out. "What's wrong here?"

"Mom, it's art. This is how you do it."

"*Ay, Dios mio,*" she said, wiping her eyeglasses. "Is this what you're learning in college?"

"This is just one of the classes."

By now more students were milling around the carrots and radishes, and even the janitor had put away his mop and was eyeing the food from a distance. There was cheese lanced with colorful toothpicks, a bowl of strawberries, and a punch bowl next to a tottering tower of Styrofoam cups.

Mom took off her glasses one more time to wipe them. She pushed her face close to a picture, as if she couldn't believe what she was seeing. It was a woman lounging in a lawn chair, legs slightly apart, and a crown of really kinky hair showing. A pool gleamed in the background, and a man in an apron cooking burgers was standing naked, his pale bottom to us.

"*¡Cochino!*" she scolded me. "You like this?"

"Mom, I didn't do it."

"Is this what you're studying?"

"I have my own style. It's different."

She didn't ask where my work was.

In one corner a student bent down to plug in a radio. A song by Creedence Clearwater Revival howled from its cracked speaker. He began to dance, and two girls joined him.

"Why can't you go into electricity? Angie's son is fixing radios and making good money." I pulled her away, but she continued, "Did you know he fixed the clock at St. John's? He got his wedding almost for free for that."

I shook my head no and led her to my drawing of striking field workers, which I had titled "*¡Huelga!*" The long dusty line of strikers curled out of view toward a sunset pink as a scar on a girl's knee. I didn't tell her that it was my drawing because I wanted her to like it a lot and then say, "This is really good, *mi'jo.* Who did this one?" But Mom wrapped her Juicy Fruit in an old coupon for Trix and said in Spanish, "*¡Mira!* These lazy people are giving us a bad name."

"Mom, they're strikers."

"*Por eso,* they have hands, don't they? Are they afraid to use them?"

Something dropped like a rock inside me. Mom didn't know anything, and I thought for a second that maybe she had peeled too many potatoes in her life to understand very much. I prodded her over to the buffet. She was happy to nibble on cheese and carrots and accept a cup of foamy punch from a cafeteria worker with a hairnet. She ate and drank and fanned herself with a paper plate. She told me that her company had sold french fries to the school for years and years, but that it had lost their account to a factory in Los Angeles.

We circled the cafeteria, drinking punch and sometimes looking at the artwork on the wall. Mom would shake her head and mumble in Spanish, "Is this what you and Abel go to school for?"

She stopped in her tracks, though, when she spotted a potted plant cowering from the lack of sun. Looking around, unsnapping her purse, she approached it slowly. Her fingers worked hungrily at tearing off a small piece of the plant to root at home.

When the coffee arrived on a cart she helped herself to that, too. She told me that college looked like fun, and I told her that we learned a lot. We were leaving just as Leslie and Glenda arrived, the baby in a tanklike stroller from Goodwill. They waved from across the cafeteria, and I waved back but didn't stop to say hello. I was glad to get to the car and say good-bye to Mom.

"No, I need you, *mi'jo*," Mom said, rolling down the window. She adjusted her pillows and said, "*Ven conmigo*. It won't take long."

We drove to her *comadre*'s house, where I was asked to climb to the roof and replace the cooler pads. I hoisted myself onto the fence and then up to the roof. With a screwdriver I pried open the side, pulled out the old pads, which broke in my hands, and stuffed in new ones. I sat for a while with my knees to my chest. I liked heights, especially roofs, because up there you can see everyone but they can't see you. Cars pulled in and out of driveways. A gang on bikes sped past. A *viejo* fiddled with his socks in the middle of his driveway. An old woman set a sprinkler on a lawn. She looked like Mrs. Garoupa but not as big. When she walked toward her house, I could hear a tinkling music in her pockets, half-pints of something. On the porch she took a bottle out, uncapped it, and swigged with gusto.

I went inside, where the air was damp with the smell of new cooler pads. Mom and her *comadre*, Martha, were in the kitchen divvying up Mom's booty of snipped leaves. Martha smiled at me and said in Spanish, "Oh, you are so strong and handsome. You want some Kool-Aid?"

"OK," I said.

After we left Mom told me she'd drop me off close to our apartment, and I thanked her for coming. Then she asked, "Which one was yours?"

"What?"

"The pictures. Which one was yours, *mi'jo?*"

I got out of the car at a busy corner, her car more in the road than alongside of it. Leaning on the window I lied and told her mine was the giraffe poking his head through the hedge. Her face brightened. She said it was beautiful, told me to be good, and drove off with her turn signal blinking right as far as I looked.

I turned into an alley, glad to get away. I kicked a rock, which scared a cat that jumped to the limbs of an apricot tree. I thought of picking the yellowing apricots, but I knew in my heart it was wrong.

I liked alleys, especially in summer. And in this alley I came across a load of abandoned aluminum, whole strips from the countertop of a restaurant. The aluminum was dull as lost spoons, but at two cents a pound it was a treasure that could get me through a week, even longer if my eyes didn't get too big. I didn't know if I should take it. But the house it came from looked abandoned. The windows were black where glass had once shone. The fruit of its loquat tree had been poked by vicious birds.

There was too much aluminum to haul at one time. I took an armful and carried it awkwardly halfway up the alley. Then I returned for a second batch. I took the first batch a little farther, my steps short and furious. Back for the second batch. I worked greedily because I knew that aluminum could bring us all that money. My chest heaved. My arms hurt. Sweat splotched my shirt and dripped from my dirty brow, which was furrowed with guilt. It wasn't stealing, but it seemed wrong to want that aluminum so badly that I would haul more than I could carry at one time. But I begged my body to keep going, and cursed everyone who would not understand that you had to do these things.

I arrived at the apartment through the back gate, exhausted, my chest pinched where the aluminum had rubbed me with hard metal and bad feelings. I piled the aluminum on the side of the house and stripped off my shirt. I ran the shirt under my arms and called, "Abel, look!" I wanted to surprise him and share some of my find with him.

Abel and Maureen came out of the apartment. They were both fresh-looking, almost beautiful. I was embarrassed standing there grimy, without my shirt on.

"Where'd you get it?" Abel was happy for me. He picked up a strip of aluminum, whistled, and said, "You're doing all right."

I beamed and put my shirt back on. Then Abel pulled me aside and said, "Jesse, can you do me a favor?" I could smell his cologne and soap, and a little of Maureen's. I could see he didn't want to ask.

"Can you take care of the baby?"

Leslie and Glenda joined us, washed and clean-looking, too. The four of them were going to go somewhere, and Abel wanted me to stay. Leslie would not look at me. He turned and twisted a loquat from the tree.

"Where are you guys going?"

Abel lowered his eyes and mumbled, "Jesse, we're just going out. Come on, man."

"Where's Mrs. Garoupa?"

"She went with a friend to bingo," Glenda said, moving from Leslie's side.

I looked at them all, standing in the shade of the garage, right behind flaps of laundry. They wanted me to say yes. They wanted to go out as couples. I was odd man out.

Because I loved my brother, because it was their turn and not mine, I nodded and said that I would be happy to take care of little Larry.

They left, and immediately the baby tripped over the pile of aluminum and started one of those cries where it takes a long time for the real crying to come out.

sixteen

abel and maureen had their chance at happiness. It looked like my turn was going to come when my high-school friend Luis Estrada drove his father's almost-new ragtop Thunderbird to our apartment and begged me to go with him to the end-of-the-year dance for seniors that night. He told me everyone was wondering what had happened to me. Someone had said I flunked out of school. My counselor figured that I went off to become a priest. Even Mrs. Otero and Mrs. Hansen in the cafeteria kitchen stirred up a batch of rumors when they pulled off their hairnets: They were sure that I was already married and a father because I was the quiet type. Coach recalled that I liked drawing pictures of the sea, so he said I had lied about my age and joined the Coast Guard.

"Come on, Jess," Luis cried. He reeked of Aqua Velva. When I asked him how come he was wearing it on a regular day, he clicked his tongue. Girls like sweet smells Monday through Friday, he said, and a double dose on the weekend.

Luis was good-looking, real brown, and his father, a man with one burn-scarred hand, owned a bakery that sweetened the air of at least two blocks in south Fresno.

"How come you dropped out of school?" he asked as he sat down on our springless couch.

I told him I wanted to get started early on college, that I wanted to become an artist. I showed him my drawing of farmworkers, and he said, "I'd hate to work like that."

Luis convinced me I should go to the dance. Rich from working two nights a week for Maureen's dad, Abel had bought me a pair of new Levi's. And Mom had bought me a shirt that was crisp as new money and just as green. So I had new clothes. But I also had a new worry—Ron Dryer might be at the dance, ready to hit me in the nose again. I was relieved when Luis told me that Ron had gotten his foot run over when the hand brake on his car had slipped. So I agreed to go, although I was nervous about seeing my classmates again.

After Luis left I pulled a handful of loquats from

Mrs. Garoupa's tree, listened to the far-off trains clanking south with their boxcars of coal and black-and-white cows, and thought about living there. I didn't miss living at home, though I did miss the home cooking and the free use of a washer and dryer. Here, with Abel, with Glenda, and now with Leslie, I felt I was with people I wanted to be with. Maybe that's why I had dropped out of school.

I bathed and brushed my hair until every loose hair parachuted to the floor and only the good ones clung to my scalp. I checked my smile in the mirror, teeth square as Chiclets and almost as white. I scrubbed the twin rings on my neck, sure they were playground dirt left over from childhood. No matter how hard I scrubbed, the rings remained. As a final touch I even went so far as to sit at the kitchen table with my dark elbows propped in halved lemons. My grandma said that the acid of lemons could bleach the dirt out and even told me a story about a man from her town in Mexico who fell asleep on a pile of lemon rinds, only to wake with half his face white, the other dark.

Early that evening Luis picked me up in his father's Thunderbird, the top down and the radio boosted pretty high. He wore a triple dose of Aqua Velva and his hair was as shiny as the chrome on the car. He was wearing white pants and a striped shirt, and sort of looked like one of the Beach Boys, but with a brown face and a nose pushed in like clay.

"I like your clothes," I said. Jealousy clawed at my heart because Luis was a rich kid, the only Mexican rich kid I knew. If I told him that I worked in the fields for my money, he might let me off at a corner and just speed away. But jealousy was a sin, and I cooled my thoughts by breathing deeply in and out.

"You look all right," Luis said kindly. He said I was sharp-looking and even the cute girls would want to dance with me.

The first thing Luis did was put some skid marks on Belmont Avenue. He flipped off some old men in old cars and raced a Ford Maverick with one cockeyed head-light that was nearly falling out of its socket. He stepped hard on the accelerator and three summer bugs splattered against the windshield as we picked up speed. When I told Luis to slow down, he yelled "This is fun!" over the engine noise, and then braked so hard that his forehead hit the steering wheel and I lifted out of my seat.

"Man, that hurt," he whined. He rubbed his forehead and laughed through the pain. He collected himself and cruised with one eye on the mirror and one on the road. He headed in the direction of Scotty's Liquor. When he skidded to a halt at a red light, I had to grab the dash-board.

"Do I have a bump on my head?" he asked, lowering his head and pushing it toward me. I saw a patch of pimples, but no bump.

"No, I don't see anything."

The red light turned green, and Luis pulled away without even looking to see if the intersection was clear.

"I don't think we should do it," I told Luis, who had said he would get someone to buy him a six-pack of beer. He snickered and said that he was surprised that I didn't know how to have fun. He said that everyone, including the good girls, drank like fish. Even the teachers were tottering in the hallways, Luis said.

At Scotty's Liquor, Luis nudged me with an elbow and said, "You can wait here or come with me."

I got out of the car and joined him. But I didn't like what we were doing. Every time a car pulled its squeaky carriage into the parking lot, I bent down and pretended to tie my shoelaces. I did this six times because none of the cars seemed to Luis banged up enough to trust. But when a ragged truck pulled in, Luis clicked his fingers, whispered, "This is the one," and approached it after the truck was parked. A beer-bellied guy in a bathing suit got out.

"Sir," I heard Luis call. Then, gesturing with his hands and looking around nervously, Luis began his story. The man nodded and Luis dug into his pockets and handed him the money. The man squeezed the money in a closed fist and went into the store. He came out with a six-pack of beer under his arm. He took two for himself, and we got four, "A fair deal," Luis said, as the car jumped out of the parking lot.

We drove to the high school; the windshield picked

up the poor souls of more summer bugs, fat with the juices of fruit and dog droppings. I wanted to tell Luis that it wasn't a good idea to buy beer from grown-ups, but it was his car and his money, and I was beginning to think that maybe I should learn, as he said, to have fun.

We parked near the school auditorium, where Luis opened a beer and took a birdlike sip. He sighed, burped softly, and smacked his lips. Then throwing his head back, he took a swig that moved his Adam's apple from top to bottom. I saw that he had twin rings circling his neck, too, and I thought maybe only Mexican people had them.

"Come on, Jess, you only live once," he said, poking an elbow in my stomach. Now I could see the bump on his forehead, his face shiny from the thrill of steering his father's car recklessly.

Smiling, I waved off his offer and got out of the car. Luis chugged on his beer and then rummaged under the seat. He brought out a bottle of Aqua Velva, splashed his throat, and wrung his hands in the stuff. Then he popped a Certs into his mouth, and we started toward the cafeteria.

The music was blaring from a stereo, where two guys in tie-dyed shirts were looking at the backs of album covers. Balloons rocked from the ceiling and streamers waved in the current of loud chatter, music, and the breeze from open windows. Two teachers leaned against the piano. One parent was smoking a cigarette by the back door. No one was dancing. They were all just standing in groups and swaying.

Luis paid my way, using a coupon, and we entered while a recording of "Under My Thumb" by the Stones was wobbling on the turntable.

"Hello, hello, hello," Luis screamed, greeting a really good-looking girl with green eyes. Her name was Julie, and I remembered seeing her fluttering around campus in lots of good clothes. She was popular, a cheerleader, an exchange student to Sweden once, a member of the student council, president of something or other, and a teen fashion model for Penney's. She had a car, too, and bought lunches she poked with a fork but didn't eat.

"Luis!" she cried sweetly, hugging him for his Aqua Velva and good looks.

Luis introduced me. She extended her hand, pumped mine, and said with surprise, "Oh, I remember you! What are you doing?"

I told her I was in junior college and began to explain that I wanted to be an artist and was living with my brother, Abel, who was either going to major in Spanish or forestry. We lived near downtown, I told her, near the courthouse, and had she ever noticed the Armenian men who played dominoes under the trees?

She looked at me, head tilted, and when her weak

smile took the shape of an O, I stopped and let Luis pull her away to the dance floor. They joined others in dancing to "96 Tears."

I poured myself a cup of pink punch and drank it on the spot. I poured myself another cup and watched Luis in his white pants and Julie in her equally white dress spin and dip to the song. They seemed happy. Everyone seemed happy, or at least busy making smiles that brightened their faces. The song ended, and when "Gimme Some Lovin'" started, Luis danced even harder.

I wandered over to the stereo, where the two guys in tie-dyed shirts were choosing the songs to play. When I told them I liked the Temptations, they glanced at me through their long hair but didn't say anything. I stayed there for a while, staring at the album covers, and then decided to say hi to Mr. Perry, the biology teacher. He was facing the wall, looking at the fire extinguisher, it seemed.

"Mr. Perry, sir," I said.

When he turned I saw that his watery eyes were as loose as the balloons on the ceiling. His bolo tie had slipped and his collar was out of whack. He was drunk, sad, and choking, I supposed, on the fact that everyone was young and having fun on punch and dance music.

"Hi," I started again. "You probably don't remember me, but I went to this school."

He smacked his dry lips, and after a moment in

which he gazed at my face, he told me yes, he remembered me and my brother, and how were things in the navy?

I told him that I wasn't in the navy, so he asked when I had gotten out. I ignored this comment. I told him that everything was OK and that I was going to City College with Abel. I told him I was in a biology class and was even getting a B. His face remained sad. I glanced around the cafeteria and said, "Nice talking with you, sir," and left, feeling bad for him.

I danced to a few songs with a girl name Inez. She said she remembered me in English class as being one of the first students to recognize the difference between adjectives and adverbs. I danced furiously after this compliment and drank more punch.

I was beginning to enjoy myself when Luis came up to me and whispered, "Hey, we're going, dude. Julie has a friend for you."

"For me?" I asked. "What do you mean?"

Shaking his head, Luis said that he was surprised that I wasn't catching on. I looked over Luis's shoulder at Julie and a girl who was large but not so large that she couldn't fit in the backseat of a Thunderbird. He pulled me over and introduced me to the girl, whose name was June. I remembered her face but nothing else about her.

We left the dance and drove around for a while, the radio blaring. At red lights Luis smothered his face into Julie's, and I thought I saw his tongue dart in and out of her puckered mouth. I felt embarrassed. I wanted to ask Luis to let me out because I had to work early the next morning, but I knew that he would click his tongue at me and say, "Come on, you only live once."

June wouldn't open up. When I looked at her, she looked away. When I looked away, she looked at me. I tried to talk to her. I asked, "How's school?" "Are you going to college?" "Do you have any brothers and sisters?" But she sat there, pudgy hands in her lap, answering each question simply and looking up at the billboards and storefronts, her eyes empty of interest.

When Luis turned on a dark road, my heart pounded and my hands gripped my new Levi's. He was heading toward the levee where Ron Dryer had hit me. The road darkened, and the moon rode freely on the canal water.

"Luis?" I called, leaning my head toward the front seats. I was nervous about this place.

"What?"

"Where are we going?"

"Calm down."

"Yeah, calm down," Julie said playfully. "Here, have some beer." She shoved a can of warm beer into my hands.

The Thunderbird kicked up a whirlwind of dust and leaves, and then skidded to a halt. Luis cut the engine and was immediately at Julie's throat. They kissed and groaned without shame. In the dark I looked at June, who was now just breathing in and out. I could sense that she was staring at me, and I didn't know what to do but say that the dance was fun.

Luis then opened his side of the door and Julie opened hers. They got out laughing and ran happily to look at the canal. I got out, too, and with some effort, June pushed herself up. The four of us stared at the water and watched a tire float past followed by a plastic bag of bread and an armada of lemon rinds. Looking beyond the trash, Julie hugged Luis and said, "Oh, it's so beautiful out here."

The wind picked up and rustled the trees. I looked down at the water fractured with moonlight, tires, and gutted lemons.

Suddenly a pair of headlights shone up the road, and I could hear the roar of an engine and the blare of a radio. I looked at Luis, whose eyes were lit with fear. He looked like a little boy in a sailor suit.

"Who are they?" Julie asked as she clung to Luis.

The car stopped in a cloud of dust. Three guys got out, and one of them was Ron Dryer with a beer in his hand. They staggered toward us, and I could see that Ron was limping. I guessed his run-over foot didn't hurt enough to keep him at home. This levee was more dangerous than I'd realized.

"Well, check this out, it's Julie, the class prez." He looked at Luis and said, "Hey, Luis, you get any?"

"Watch what you're saying!" Luis said.

"Level with us, Luis. Did you or didn't you get any?"

The three guys laughed. One of the guys unzipped his pants and wagged a tremendous stream of pee on a rock.

This angered Luis, who cussed and called the guy some names. The guy just burped and threw his empty beer can into the canal to join the flow of lemon rinds.

Ron burped, too, and then hit Luis in the nose. For a moment I saw myself stagger back holding my nose while yellow stars of pain shot inside my head. I saw myself take a swing at Ron and Ron hitting me three times. I saw myself drop to a knee with the first salty rush of blood dripping into the thirsty earth. I saw myself shamed in front of girls who were hugging each other and crying. But it wasn't me. It was Luis and his white pants that were now catching some of the blood that ran as red as the night was black.

seventeen

now more spooked than ever, I decided to keep my distance from the levee. I also decided to stay away from Luis Estrada. He had bled a lot that night, and I bled a little when I helped him out. I had felt pretty good hitting Ron Dryer, watching blood leap from his freckled face to his shirt, pants, and cowboy boots. I smacked him once and twisted his ears when he picked me up and gave me a bear hug. But there were three of them and only two of us, not counting the crying girls with runny mascara. It was a tough night of bloodletting and awful cussing.

I decided to spend the last weeks of spring semester working hard. I gave up on Minerva. I gave up on Raul and his group. My only real interest was art, and Mr. Helperin announced that for extra credit we could do any project remotely connected to art.

I mulled this over because I knew that my grade was between a B and an A, possibly closer to a B. I knew I could probably do another drawing and get credit, but a week earlier I had thumbed through a book on Asian art and came across a chapter on bonsai, the art of re-shaping little trees. I liked their ancient look. And they reminded me of wind-swept trees on the coast.

Early one Saturday morning I decided to pull a small sapling from the pine grove in the courthouse park. Abel lay in bed, his face smothered in morning shadows and dank bedroom air. I dressed and left the apartment, the streetlight pale against the sky. I didn't like doing this and prayed for forgiveness as I walked around the pine. On my third turn I leaped toward the sapling. I dug it up, placed it in a cardboard box, and hurried home, my arms weighed down with wet earth and sin.

"What are you doing?" Abel asked. He was slapping a pair of dirty socks against a kitchen chair, getting rid of their stiffness. He had to be at work by nine.

"It's for extra credit," I told him, explaining that bon-sai is an ancient Japanese art form of twisting little trees so that they look old in a matter of weeks. I told him about the extra credit.

"It's a good deal," he said. He sat down and put on his socks. "Where did you get it?"

I was afraid he'd ask. I didn't want Abel to think that I went around stealing, but if I lied, then I would sin two times in one day.

"At the courthouse," I finally told Abel. "I'm going to put it back when I get done."

He turned without saying anything and opened the refrigerator. He stared at two apples, cheese, a gallon of milk, and three eggs. He asked, "You eat breakfast?"

"I had some cereal," I said.

He brought out two eggs and weighed them in the flat of his palms. He brought out the other egg, turning it over. He had boiled one of them. He looked at them closely before he cracked two over a black frying pan. It turned out the one in his left hand had been boiled. He put it back in the refrigerator and ate leaning against the kitchen sink. Maureen's Volkswagen tooted from the curb.

I took my pine sapling to the back porch. The sun was bright and birds were fooling in the loquat tree, sinking their beaks into the sweet pulp. I brought out a spool of copper wire, pulled out a good length, and snipped it with a pair of pliers. Then I repotted the sapling in a Folger's coffee can and fed it water from a Coke bottle. I talked to it. I told the sapling, "You're going to be OK. I'm going to put some wire on you, and you're going to look great."

I heard Mrs. Garoupa fiddling with the door to her back porch. She came out sweeping. When she saw me she asked, "What are you doing, Jesse?"

"A school project," I answered.

She climbed down her back porch and onto our porch for a closer look at the sapling. She examined it and concluded, "That's a sad twig." She touched a limb, and some needles rained down.

"I gave it some water," I said.

"You need fertilizer."

She returned to her porch, pushed a hand into a bag, and came back with a pile of white grains. She sprinkled the grains in the can and said, "This should help." Then she said, "You need a haircut, Jesse. Your brother, too."

I touched my hair and said, "I like it like this."

"I know it's none of my business, but are you a hippie?" She was concerned. "A good-looking boy like you shouldn't have long hair. You'll use up all your hair if you grow it all now."

I reassured her that I wasn't a hippie. Looking over her shoulder I saw baby Larry tottering out the back door with two crayons in his mouth. She turned and followed my gaze. She yelled, "Cut that out," and slapped her thigh. "That's nasty." Baby Larry threw the crayons, turned, and backed into the edge of the door, hard. He started one of his cries, the tears flowing long before the noise came.

After Mrs. Garoupa left I found my Asian art book,

flipped through the pages of the bonsai section, and ate the hard-boiled egg that Abel had left me. I wound the wire tightly but carefully around the three puny limbs. Still more needles fell.

I bent the wire so that the limbs were caught in a wind-blown gesture. The sapling looked like a prisoner. I felt sorry for the plant and placed it in the shade. I perked up when I heard a knock at the front door.

I hurried through the kitchen and pulled open the door. It was Luis, my high-school friend, wearing a clean pair of white pants and looking pretty nicely dressed for a Saturday morning.

"Hey, Jesse," Luis greeted me. He was carrying some books and papers.

"Come on in," I said, pulling back the screen door.

He looked around and said, "Thanks for helping out."

He meant during the fight at the levee. I told Luis that's what friends are for. I told him that I was really glad to hit Ron. Even if it wasn't right, it had to be done.

Luis sat down and said shyly, "I'm applying to college. I need your help with the application."

"I don't know anything about college."

"But you're in college now!"

I said, "I mean I don't know anything about the forms and things. Abel helped me."

"Is Abel here?"

"No, he's at work."

Luis sighed and slapped the papers against his clean pants. "Damn, I have to get this in the mail by Monday. They already gave me an extension."

"Where are you applying?"

"Berkeley."

He showed me an application loaded with tiny print. I only knew how to fill out the parts that ask your name and where you live. I didn't know anything about financial matters or SAT scores. I used some of my speed-reading, though, and in a matter of seconds I realized that Luis was five months late in applying.

"Well, maybe I can help on the personal essay," I suggested. I looked at the application one more time and then at Luis. I knew he wasn't smart. He had been in my history class during my junior year, and more than once I had had to tell him that Benjamin Franklin wasn't ever president and that it was Roosevelt, not Jefferson, on the dime. Still, he was a friend. I asked him what he wanted to do with his life. He fidgeted in his seat and said that he would like to help his people.

"What people?" I asked.

"Mexican people, man."

Luis didn't act Mexican, so his answer caught me off guard. I always thought of him as a brown surfer, he looked so cool, so unsweaty. I clicked my tongue and asked, "What else?"

"What else what?"

"Is there anything else you want to do?"

"I want to make money—lots! I'm tired of working at the bakery."

"It's not that bad."

"How do you know? I always smell like a batch of *pan dulce*."

I sighed and said, "OK, let's get to work." We moved from the living room to the kitchen. He told me about himself and his merchant family, and where his father was from in Mexico. I wrote it all down, wrote out his years as a soccer player, his one year as an altar boy, his likes and dislikes, his favorite people, including presidents and actors, and finally how he loved cars. He said he wanted the university people to know that he had a mechanical mind because he intended to major in engineering. He thought it might help.

I wrote out his personal essay once and then copied it carefully a second time, using plenty of looping action in my script because I thought it would make Luis seem lively and confident. He was amazed when I explained the difference between *it's* and *its*. When he finally caught on, he said he wished he had quit high school to start college early like me. He told me I was really smart and a good guy for helping him fight Ron Dryer. He thanked me, said three times he would remember me forever, and left with a skip in his step.

I returned to my bonsai and discovered more needles had been let loose. I moved it inside to the kitchen counter and fiddled with the wires. I cooed, "Come on, little guy." I sprinkled coffee grounds into the soil, a home remedy that I had watched Mom use on sick plants and weak soil.

On Sunday the plant looked worse, and by Tuesday, the day of my art class, the bonsai was nearly bald, the needles lying like pickup sticks around the pot.

"It looks bad," Abel remarked over a bowl of shredded wheat. He ate and got dressed, and I got dressed but didn't eat because I wanted to suffer along with my bonsai. *It's all my fault,* I told myself, and carried the potted plant to school. Leslie walked with us, quiet because he knew that I wasn't feeling good about my extra-credit project.

I went to Phys Ed first and then to art studio. When I brought my bonsai into class, Mr. Helperin was smoking a cigarette and looking at his grade book. He blew smoke at the book and then looked up at me and asked, "What do you have there, Jesse?"

"It's a bonsai. It's for extra credit." I placed it in front of him. It was now just three bald and shackled limbs, apparently dead to light, water, and any kind of music that might perk it up. I explained the Asian art book I had read and my feelings about taking nature and re-shaping it. I told him it was a pine and when I had gotten it. I told him why the Japanese liked small things. He nodded at me and said that art can sometimes be deadly. He opened his roll book and made a check for extra credit.

After class when I returned to the apartment, feeling lousy for my bonsai, I discovered a bag on our porch. At first I thought it was from Mom, but I knew better when I read: "Your nice friend forever. Its in the mail my dad says." I peeked in the grease-splotched bag and took out a turtle-shaped *pan dulce*. I took a bite, and the sweetness worked its glory on my back molars. I ate two, and then I unwound the wire from my bonsai, freeing its tortured limbs now that my grade had moved from a B to an A.

eighteen

abel and i never made it to the sea, but after spring semester was a done deal, our textbooks tossed in the closet, my fine for a lost combination lock paid, and John Philip Sousa marched away into memory, Leslie drove me to Piedra River. The river was twenty miles outside of Fresno, where the sky thinned to shreds of good air and the light sprang off every living and dead leaf. We brought along two inner tubes and plenty of sandwiches and drinks. We ate in the shade of the cottonwood, neither of us bothered much by pesky gnats, glad to be done with school. Glad to dangle one foot over sand and the other in water. These were good choices, and so were the sandwiches: ham or tuna bought with the earnings from my aluminum.

Water roared from Pine Flat Dam's six chutes, and the birds were either deaf, hard of hearing, or simply foolish, but they seemed to like singing for their own sweet pleasure while mist dripped from their beaks. They were mostly nervous finches. We stood facing the dam, faces wet, and I thought if the dam suddenly broke, I would finally get my wish and end up at the sea.

We sang because we were free of school. We climbed one side of the dam, rocks crumbling away under our shoes, and our faces and arms damp from the spray. We climbed the slant of earth, and at the top we admired the foothills dotted with cows and oaks and moss-flecked boulders. We admired the dam, which was more cement than two eyes can take in at one time.

"What ever happened to that girl you liked?" Leslie asked.

I let dirt pour like time from my palm. I wasn't sure if he meant Minerva or Lupe. I shrugged and answered, "I don't know how to get a girlfriend."

Leslie chuckled and said, "You're too much."

"You and Abel have girls, and I don't."

"You're going to have to beat them off with a stick."

Leslie's face was wet with mist and sweat. His hurt eye was golden in the sunlight. I said with a sigh, "It would be nice."

"You're going to have lots. Don't worry."

We climbed down slowly with bone-colored sticks as our staffs, our shoes kicking up clouds of dust. A terrible joy swayed in my body because I knew I could tumble and scrape myself on rock and thistle. I looked at my palms. If I fell, they would bleed from trying to hold on.

At the river's edge we set our inner tubes on the water and entered the icy current one step at a time. We lowered ourselves onto the tubes, butts down, legs sticking skyward. We paddled, splashed, and screamed "Holy Lord" more because it was cold than because it was scary. Leslie told me to be careful, to take the white water slowly, and to kick toward the bank if I should flip over. I nodded, wiggled my soaked tennies, and asked, "Do you think this is snow water?"

Leslie smiled. I let my inner tube find its current to cut through, following Leslie's lead. I sang for a while, but when I fell behind I shut my mouth and got to work. I paddled furiously with my hands, watchful of jagged rocks, sticks, and fish lines, for the sudden waterfall-like dips where you could be sucked under as quick as a snap of your fingers.

I craned my neck at kids on the bank eating hot dogs. I waved like a beauty queen on her float and tried to look calm. I was glad when I caught up to Leslie and had enough strength left in my cheeks to smile and say, "This is fun, huh?"

We moved toward white water, and before Leslie could say "Be cool," we were gone, our tubes jumping up and down as if they were alive. We screamed and gripped the tubes because the river was suddenly more scary than cold. The bank seemed to pull away. I rolled and dipped and bounced and more than once almost tipped over. But just as the current had caught us, it let us go. We slowed to a lazy glide, and the gnats that we'd left on shore now buzzed around our faces for whatever it is that they like.

We paddled for a while, Leslie saying, "Man oh man, that was fun," and cold as I was, I agreed by jabbing my fist into the air. But when I saw a circle of shore that looked soft, I paddled for it. Leslie followed. I walked out of the water shivering and shook a leg. I threw myself on the warm sand, and Leslie brought out a sandwich from a plastic bag that he'd carried safely all the way.

"Here, it'll make you warm," he said.

"What do you mean?" I asked doubtfully. "A sandwich ain't a blanket."

"No, but it's energy."

Leslie explained that food is like the gas in a heater, and if you eat something real quick and then walk around, you can be warm in less than a minute. So I gobbled the sandwich and jumped around, kicking my legs to my chest. Leslie laughed, and I had to laugh, too, because the sandwich had held only a thin piece of bologna. How much energy could it contain?

"You look silly," Leslie said.

"I'm happy. I'm done with school!"

We shot the rapids six more times, and each time I grew more adventurous. I rode without holding on and then rode with my eyes closed. I rode on my belly and rode eating a sandwich the final time because I was frozen to the bone. Then I lay in the sun and Leslie sat near me, whittling a stick.

I opened an eye and asked, "What are you making?"

"A cane for Mrs. Garoupa," he answered as the blade peeled downward on the bumpy stick.

"You must like Glenda," I said.

"Very much."

"Do you love her?"

He stopped and held up the stick. "Yes, I do. That's why I'm making this cane."

A bird flitted by, a mockingbird, I thought. When I followed its flight some sun got into my eyes and startled me. I closed my eyes and asked, "Was it scary in Vietnam?"

I heard the knife rake the stick three times before Leslie answered, "I scared myself there."

"What do you mean, Leslie?"

My eyes were open now and I stared at a sky that I thought might be bluer than heaven.

"I mean, I shot at people, Jesse."

"Did you hit people?"

"I think so. I'm sorry for it."

I wondered how you could kill someone. I asked, "Are you really sorry, Leslie?"

"Yeah, I am. It was a mistake. I was your age, no, Abel's age, when they sent me over."

I rolled onto my back and sighed for all those who have to run for their lives. All my life I'd tried not to hurt people in deep ways. You didn't have to go to Vietnam to find fear. You can find it at school or on the corner. Just bumping some guy behind you by accident. This happened to Carlos, a pretty nice guy at high school, when he was buying a milkshake at Dairy Queen. He turned away from the window and stepped on someone's shoe. The next thing he knew he was holding a shake in one hand and his shoulder with the other where a knife had gone in and out without his hardly knowing.

We returned to Fresno, exhausted, sore, and once again blazing from the heat of summer. We rolled the inner tubes into Leslie's shed and ran the garden hose over our bodies to rid ourselves of sand and the smell of river water.

When we entered the apartment squeaking in soggy shoes and calling "Abel!" I was startled to see pieces of arms, legs, and heads all over the couch. A whole torso stood in a corner, and some feet were poking out from underneath the kitchen table. For a moment I thought, *Who got hurt?* but then I realized that they were limbs from Maureen's dad's work. Abel was in the kitchen with a paintbrush in one hand and a plastic forearm in the other. He was working with his shirt off.

"What's going on, Abel?" I asked. "This is really strange."

"Come on, help me," Abel said, rising to his feet.

Thanks to Maureen's dad, he explained, he had gotten extra work painting mannequins for Gottschalk's Department Store. He had to finish them by tomorrow, and he was getting twenty dollars for each mannequin.

"Easy money," Leslie said, and took up a brush and a plaster hand. He turned the hand over and then scratched his back with it.

"Do we have to put them together?"

"No, we just paint them."

I took up a brush, slapped the harshness from its bristles against my wrist, dipped it into the paint, and took up a faceless head. While I carefully stroked a pair of eyebrows on it, I told Abel about the river and how I nearly tipped over nine different times. I told him how a sandwich could warm a body and asked if it ever occurred to him that the dam might just bust open while you're standing admiring it?

"Sounds like you dudes had fun."

"Lots of fun," I said. "You should come next time."

We painted in silence until I had finished three heads. "Beats field work," I said.

Abel agreed as he shook a bottle of paint. He asked

me, "Are you going to summer school? You said you might."

"No, I'm gonna look for a job."

"How 'bout you, Leslie?"

Abel painted, and then got up to open the window, where a fly was frisking the dusty corners for something to eat. He turned on the radio, and we listened to the Doors, who were in the middle of "Light My Fire."

"Yeah, I like that song," Leslie said. "Even had the forty-five of it." Leslie was singing the words, but quiet enough not to ruin the song for us.

"You know what my favorite song was," I said, getting up from my knees and stretching, "when I was a kid?"

"What?"

"Don't laugh."

They stopped their painting and looked at me, smiles already twitching at the corners of their mouths.

"Remember 'We Gotta Sink the Bismarck'?"

They laughed from way down deep and laughed even harder when I told them I was kidding and that my real favorite song—honest-to-God this time—was "96 Tears."

The laughter fell to smiles and then simply a nice glow among us. I painted the eyebrows and thought of Minerva, whose plucked eyebrows looked like seagulls in flight. Then I painted the mouth, which was more of a dot than a line. Lupe's mouth was like that, I remembered, and her lashes were long and thick with mascara. I blushed the cheeks, and when Leslie got up and looked at my work, I said, "That was a lot of fun, huh, Leslie?"

"Sure was," he said. He was painting the fingernails. He blew on the crimson nails and set the painted hand in the doorway to dry.

"I have something to say." Abel licked his lips, his head lowered like a dry flower. He dipped his brush into black and was painting an ear hole when he said calmly, "I got my letter. Second one."

The house creaked, and it wasn't God. The window rattled, the faucet dripped into a plate, and a fly whipped itself at the window. None of it was God.

"No." Leslie sighed.

"Yeah, it came today."

My brush rolled from my hand, and the red paint at my knee spilled. I looked at my brother. "No, Abel, don't say that."

The fly in the window was circling the head of a mannequin facing the ceiling, eyes wide open in the pointless light.

nineteen

i talked with Jesus on the steps of his over-the-garage apartment and told him Abel had been drafted. Jesus listened without looking at me. I told him I just wanted to be good. If I did everything everyone told me, I thought, I would get a job and live quietly. I said César Chávez is a good man, and he would make things better for all of us. Jesus listened, his ear tilted toward my sadness, and squeezed my shoulder in a way that made me feel good. I picked at a sliver in my palm. I thought Abel let himself get drafted. He could have gone to Canada, like one guy we knew, or he could have filed some papers downtown saying why he thought it was wrong to go to war. But Abel said that it was better this way, he could serve seventeen months and be home not for this Christmas but the one after.

"I feel for you," Jesus said. "*Damn* army! It's our *raza* defending this country, and what do we get? *Nada!*"

I asked for Jesus's advice. I told him I might join the army to be with Abel, but he started shaking his head before I was finished. I said I could join Abel in South Carolina, where he was stationed, and we could sleep in the same room—Abel in the top bunk and me in the lower bunk.

Jesus shook his head, and we got up and went into his apartment. In the kitchen he poured me a glass of grape Kool-Aid, and I drank it slowly. He said I should stay in school. He swatted at a fly circling in a dusty shaft of summery light. The war would soon be over, and Abel would be home soon, he said.

Jesus squeezed my shoulder just before I left, and a shock of faith worked in my flesh. I walked up the street, hot patches of sunlight cutting through the sycamores. I walked to the courthouse. I sat on the bench and then lay down, my hands behind my head. It's a good way to see the summer sky, white as an eggshell in this heat, and it's a good way to pick up the occasional slants of wind. I thought of Abel, gone two weeks. He was probably in line for food or perhaps marching in boots with mirrory light at the tips. He could be doing sit-ups, sweat pooling in the pockets of his stomach. He had written me two letters, one in really bad Spanish and one in English. Both said the same thing: it was hot in South Carolina, and he longed for *frijoles*. Maureen told me he'd written the same thing to her and that he missed her and me, too.

I rolled from my back to my stomach, put my cheek against the bench, and let my hands dangle. I spied an ant as lean as a shadow and just as frail dragging a white thing in its jaws. It tugged and pulled, working its way over cracks in the sidewalk. I blew on the ant, which gripped the ground even harder because, it seemed, it had to get the white thing back to its hole. I closed my eyes and saw a labor bus and a worker's face smothered by a red potato sack. I saw another worker sharpening the blade of a hoe with a rock. His hands were root-colored and his face lined from the sweat that coursed down his face.

After a while I got up and started home. Home was no longer our old apartment. I couldn't afford the rent, so Leslie and I had traded places. Glenda and Leslie moved into the apartment, which angered Mrs. Garoupa at first but later made her happy because she could see that it was love, not the simple convenience of a roof over their lovemaking. But Leslie was upset. I could see in his ruined eye that he felt he was stealing from me, and I could see that Glenda was upset, too. She was sorry that Abel had been drafted, sorry that she'd ever flirted with him, sorry that I had to live in the shed with a bad door.

When I got home Mrs. Garoupa was sitting on the lawn watching baby Larry splash in the plastic blow-up pool I had found in the alley. The pool, like the baby, was patched on all its tiny punctures. Larry was sucking on the garden hose.

"Hey, baby," I cooed as I passed.

He choked and coughed, and when he looked up and saw me, he screamed, "Hi!" He was beginning to say things that made sense.

I bent down, tugged a fistful of grass, and rained the blades of grass on the surface of the water. Larry looked at the grass blades, mystified by their appearance. He said, "Hi! Hi!" and spanked the grass to the bottom of the pool.

I went to my shed, my books lined up near the washer and dryer and the soldierly stand of detergents and bleaches. My artwork hung on the south wall, where you could put a hand at five in the afternoon and feel the heat that pressed on us all day. I had our radio and records, and I had my clothes in an open-faced cardboard box. I had posters, too, and an ice chest where I kept my milk, cheese, eggs, and my occasional trophy-tall sodas.

Sleepy, I lay in bed with my hands behind my neck. It was nothing like lying on a park bench. Here, in the shed, the dead air of summer gathered in the corners. I had some sunlight at three in the afternoon. I had spiders, swirls of dust knee-high, and blue-black flies ticking against the windowpane. I had boredom splashing from the faucet and the sadness of my two pairs of shoes moored under my bed.

I slept a little and rose with sweat on my face. Dusk appeared at the window. For weeks I had wondered whether I should join the army now that I was eighteen, or if I should pick cantaloupes in Huron. Jesus had decided it for me. It was crazy to join the army, and Abel would get really angry at me if he saw me climb off the recruiting bus with my suitcase. So it would be the labor bus instead. It would be cantaloupes from late June to mid-July, cantaloupes sighing from the heat as their lopsided heads lay half-hidden behind leaves and the blur of sweat in my eyes.

I left the shed and drank from the garden hose. I washed my face there, the salt of the day running into my mouth. I unlaced my shoes, peeled off my socks, and walked around in the pool, the coolness running in chills up my back, it felt so good.

Mrs. Garoupa came out of her apartment clip-clopping in zoris with Larry in tow. She smiled at me, and Larry hurried down, tripped, rose, and joined me in the pool. I took his pudgy fist in mine, and we circled the water three times, kicking up small waves. Then I picked him up and handed him back to Mrs. Garoupa.

I was out of work and nearly out of money. I slipped

back into my shoes and started home because Mom said I should come over more often. She cried when Abel left, and even our stepfather stubbed his cigarette in his sombrero ashtray and rose from his recliner to drive Abel to the bus station.

More lonely than ever, I walked toward the court-house, now filling slowly with the dark of evening. I sat on the bench and thought of Lupe and Minerva. I imagined both of them driving away in long, shiny cars. I closed my eyes, hands over my face. Glenda and Leslie paraded inside my head. Baby Larry was peeling off a bandage. Abel lay in his bunk with a small transistor radio at his ear. Mom was cracking an egg into a bowl. In his recliner my stepfather was setting his wristwatch by the clock on the television. No one was smiling, and no one was getting up to set the crooked world straight.

I opened my eyes and ran a hand over my tears. A squirrel came down the tree to stare at me with its liquid eyes full of disease and hate. Even at this hour I could see what was coming: the fields running for miles with cantaloupes like heads, all faceless in the merciless sun.

READER CHAT PAGE

1. What problems do Jesse and Abel avoid by living on their own rather than with their mother and stepfather? What problems do they introduce?

2. Why does Jesse think it is a bad idea for Abel to get involved with Glenda?

3. What does Jesse have in common with Leslie, the Vietnam veteran?

4. What are some of the occupational hardships suffered by field-workers like Jesse and Abel?

5. Why does Jesse hesitate to get involved with *la causa* when Raul first invites him to participate in a strike?

6. Abel advises Jesse that "love comes with a price." What does Jesse experience that makes him believe this is true?

7. Having left high school a year early to attend community college, Jesse feels he is in a sort of limbo. What happens that makes him believe he belongs in college? What happens that makes him feel he was not yet ready to leave high school?

8. Jesse's mother says of the strikers, "These lazy people are giving us a bad name." How does her attitude make Jesse feel? How does Jesse's attitude about strikers differ from hers?